Alone with a Man in a Room

Shaun Levin

ALSO BY SHAUN LEVIN

Seven Sweet Things

Snapshots of The Boy

A Year of Two Summers

Isaac Rosenberg's Journey to Arras

Trees at a Sanatorium

Alone with a Man in a Room

Kiss and Tell Press, June 2021

kissandtellpress.com

"The Beautiful Boy" first appeared in *With: New Gay Fiction*. Ed. Jameson Currier. Chelsea Station Editions, 2013. "I Will Tell this Story" appeared in *Who's Yer Daddy?* Eds. Jim Elledge and David Groff. Wisconsin University Press, 2012. "Foreigners in Sitges" appeared in *Best Gay Erotica 2012*. Ed. Richard Labonte. Cleis Press, 2012. "The Homo Daddy's Guide to Lovemaking" appeared in *Daddies*. Ed. Richard Labonte. Cleis, 2008. "Three French Men" appeared in *I Like It Like That*. Eds. Richard Labonte and Lawrence Schimel. Arsenal Pulp Press, 2009. "Jack Kerouac Is the Buddha" appeared in *Callisto*. Ed. Raymond Luczak. Sibling Rivalry Press, 2017. "The Man in the Pool" first appeared in *Flamingo Land*. Ed. Ellah Wakatama Allfrey. Flight Press, 2015. "Not Alone Enough" appeared in *After Words*. Ed. Kevin Bentley. Alyson Books, 2001. "The Smell of Asparagus Pee" appeared in *Gay Times Book of Short Stories*. Ed P-P Hartnett. Gay Times Books, 2000 and later in *Boyfriends from Hell*. Ed. Kevin Bentley. Green Candy Press, 2003 "The Myths of this Place" appeared in *Love, Christopher Street*. ed. Thomas Keith. Vantage Point, 2012. "Leaving Tel Aviv" was firt published as "The Last City I Loved: Tel Aviv" on therumpus. net, June 2012. "Some Hasidic Tales." appeared in *Brand* (Summer 2007). Eds. Nina Rapi and Cherry Smyth. "Frozen Years" was first published in *Chelsea Station*, Edition 1, November 2011.

Cover image: iStock.com/Nevskyphoto

This is a work of fiction.

ISBN 978-1-912277-22-3

For the thousand men who've said yes:
without you, this book would not exist

Contents

Introduction

Many of these pieces have been with me for so long I can't remember whether they're fact or fiction. Most are probably a combination of the two. I remember the time and place of their conception: those sweltering afternoons in London writing in an overgrown Abney Park Cemetery, a trip to Lille for writing and sex, the holiday in Almería on my way to Fundación Valparaíso for a writing retreat. Some pieces have been incomplete for so long, they'll remain in a state of becoming forever.

This book is a love letter to London and Tel Aviv, a stock-taking of work that has accumulated over the past twenty years. It's a farewell card and a thank-you note, a restrospective of stories and essays written in the first twenty years of this new century.

Shaun Levin
Madrid, June 2021

The Beautiful Boy

And so we all began to walk behind the beautiful boy, some of us more confidently than others. We didn't care what others thought, how we appeared to those who saw us. So what if we were old and fat and ugly? We'd do whatever it took to get the boy to notice us. We'd stare and stare as if the force of our desire was enough to ignite his. We lived in hope, because you can never tell when a beautiful boy will say "yes." It's hard to know what the young and beautiful want until you hear a "no" or "no, thank you" or have your hand eased away from a knee. Some of us have heard "no" so many times that one more "no" is no big deal, not if there's a slight possibility – in every situation there's a possibility – that the beautiful boy will say "yes." He might let us touch or stroke, might let us watch. He might let us kiss his back or shoulder, the nape of his neck, right there, turning his head away just a fraction. He might let us kneel before him to accept what he has to offer.

We are happy to follow a boy like him in the knowledge that we might get a furtive touch, a glance. We have known boys happy to be watched, and for some of us that is enough. We don't care that his beauty is clichéd – tall and lean and smooth, though we've noticed he trims his chest and can tell a substantial covering would emerge if only he'd let it grow, which a few of us would like very much, and for that reason, for the echo of his manly chest, we like him even more than we would have had he been as smooth as the boy he appears to be. But on the whole, we're not picky.

We follow the beautiful boy along the labyrinths of this place, its black walls, exposed brickwork, the lights opaque, some a murky yellow, others a dim green or red, too feint to cast shadows, yet bright enough to cloud our vision, especially that green light at the end of the passage, so that when you walk towards it, other men become silhouettes, and for a moment you fear you'll collide with the one walking towards you or the one leaning against the wall as he waits for the right man to come along.

We aren't sure what kind of man the beautiful boy is after, for we've seen boys like him – some even more beautiful – who've been intimate, even very intimate, with men much older, fatter or uglier than us. So we keep walking. Some of us fear he might stop in his tracks at any moment and cause a pile-up of lecherous bodies on the dark linoleum floor, like a traffic accident or those beached whales, washed up for some unknown reason, stuck on the wet sand as waves dab water onto them, then slowly recede as the tide goes out and the fat creatures are left to die.

This place is not a beach, though we are always naked under our towels, and there is somewhere to swim, and we have escaped our day-to-day existence to be here, the way one escapes to the sea.

The beautiful boy leads us along the corridors, past open cabins where men sit and wait to be approached. One or two of us stop to try our luck, the rest of us keep walking, following the boy, his back sculpted into a V-shape, the cleft of his spine like a furrow from neck to clean white towel wrapped tightly across his buttocks. Down the stairs, and up another flight to where the jacuzzi is, and the steam room and the swimming pool that is big enough for four or five strokes, just the right size for two laps underwater. Some of us have done that before, maybe not lately, but we remember having done it, holding our breath as we swam from one end to the other, then back again, partly to impress, and partly for the exhilaration of being naked in public and weightless in water.

As if he'd been reading our thoughts, the beautiful boy stands by the chrome ladder at the edge of the pool, moves closer to skim his toe across the surface. The temperature is pleasing to him, so he unfurls his towel and drapes it across the railings while we stare, even those of us who are not at an angle to see the front of him, though most of us crane our necks to catch a glimpse. He pauses for a moment at the edge of the pool, as if to offer us one last glimpse, and we all think of the wonderful phrase "semi-erect," as the beautiful boy lowers himself into the water.

No matter how many times we experience it, beauty is unfathomable. It delights and surprises, every discovery as if we've chanced upon it for the first time, every encounter a re-encountering of that first boy we were awed by, silenced by, whom we shadowed in the playground, whose marbles we fetched, for whom we took swimming lessons just to be close to. We wore the same clothes, went to his house to play, invented reasons to sleep over, and at night we dreamed of him, of being him, or so like him that no one could tell us apart, until we were told... by whom? The knowledge filtered into us through the air, through the gaze of history, telling us we were not worthy of one so beautiful, not worthy of such proximity. This is part of our inner mechanism, even if the exact point in our youths when the seed of shame was planted is now lost, it's a view that has shaped us, especially when we are so close to one as beautiful as the boy.

We watch him swim short laps, his body clear and gleaming, skin shining as his back and shoulders rise above the surface. Those of us who've waded in after him, make conversation as if conversation is all we want.

The boy is gracious, unfazed by our advances, never reciprocating. We hope he might be Brazilian, most of us have met Brazilians who like older men, so different to the rude young men who grow up in the West, haunted by youth even when they are young. Perhaps he is Greek or Romanian, but we can't be sure, nor can we be sure how exactly men from those parts of the world feel about men who are old and fat and ugly.

While the boy showers, we peer at him like boys spying through a hole in the wall at a man undressing. Some of us guess him to be twenty-five, though it is hard to tell, he could be younger or older. We don't care. We are happy just to watch the shower-water as it lands on his skin, the soap froth and drain from his chest and middle, the quiet way he returns to his towel hanging on its hook as if waiting to have life breathed back into it. There are more of us now, and we follow the beautiful boy into the steam room. It is small and we have to stand close together. Some of us don't like this. We don't want the man next to us to think we are brushing against him out of desire.

We are an audience to the boy and his beauty, following him with our eyes as he approaches the man who has been sitting on the ledge since before we entered, us, the entourage of the beautiful boy. The boy sits down as if to rest, he's worked the hardest, led us through narrow corridors, across a pond, through the showers to finally reach this point where he has found another man to come to the fore, this man whom he turns to with a look in his eyes that says: "You lead now. You call the navigational shots."

The man's chest is covered with dark wet hair, his manhood soft and thick between his legs, the hair above it – abundant. Some of us, seeing how desiring the boy is of the man feel a pang of reassurance, there was a time when we looked like the man, graceful, handsome. The word "virile" comes to mind. We have all been virile. The man looks at us, smiles as if he can tell who we've been and who we are and that pleases him. He rises from his ledge and walks towards us and his breath is warm and his hands are warm and his touch is gentle, his mouth – soft, his embrace – strong, his voice confident as he whispers the question one asks a man one is in pursuit of: Are you alone?

And we nod our heads yes. Yes, we're alone. And he kisses us, every one of us, from the tall man with the belly to the short Spaniard whose bald-patch is round and shining. The rest of us press against the man and he hugs us and we hug him and feel our soft bellies against his firm stomach, kiss him passionately, the way he kisses us. Our eyes flit around the room, moving from man to man, taking in our faces and our beards, our chins, our hair, the sturdiness of our backs, the strength of our arms, the distances we've covered and how we've survived. Occasionally we catch glimpses of the beautiful boy perched on the ledge watching us as we touch the man but mostly we touch each other, discovering something new, or something we'd forgotten, and we hold and stroke and kiss each other as if we've wanted this for a long time, and in that time have dreamt of each other, and now we're together again.

We can't all remember when we saw the beautiful boy leave. Some of us say, yes, of course, he did leave, because we've heard the story told over and over about how he stepped off his perch and hovered amongst us, moved through us, his body sleek and glowing, his cheeks reddened by the heat, his skin against ours, the curve of his back and buttocks, the leanness of his abdomen, the heft of his manhood. Then he was at the door and he turned to watch us – that's what some of us saw – but it was as if, by then, we'd changed direction mid-flight, and no one could be sure whether the boy had left or he's still with us, swooping and gliding through the sky, moving to some invisible rhythm, beyond words or reason. And us, we're all lighter and younger and more beautiful than we've ever been, and the boy is amongst us, sometimes in front, sometimes moving alongside us, his body held up by the vortex of our wings.

One Two Three

Saturday

Do you belong here?

Of course not, I say. But I *live* here.

What she wants to know is whether these are my people, if I have the *right* to be here, a question asked of all immigrants, all not-from-heres, when the time comes to determine who'll stay and who must go.

Then she – we're talking about my mother – goes back to where she came from, not to where she's from, because we left that place long ago, but to where she came from to be with me, here in this city that shelters us both from the wars we've got ourselves into. Now I'm alone in this room in this hotel.

What compels a man to book into a hotel in a city that is his, but is not where he is from. *His* city, because there are places he feels ownership of. A park. A gym. A cycle route. A man says: It's my city. This city is mine. Not in the way this pen is mine or this notebook, not in the way that mother is mine or that father (deceased), the way you were mine. And this room is mine. For the duration of my stay, for these three days that I have paid to be here, this room is mine. And me, am I mine? In the neutral space of a hotel room, in its quiet anonymity, undetectable, I am nobody's.

I is the singular. I is itself.

I is eye and one is won. Who put the past tense of win in one? Once upon a time I was one. I won! Rare, but it's been done, a prefect in junior school, house captain. But the story I tell is of a boy on his own, and then along comes another (sister) and another (brother). One plus one, plus one. To play alone for two years is a long time, so long that one could assume it has been like this forever and so it has been. Like this. Forever. Playing alone, dreading the next one, and then: no longer to be the one but to be one of two, of three. (Actually, four.)

A man leaves his hotel room for food, energy for the things he's about to do. Soon he will bump into people he likes, friends; he'll be eating his sandwich by the river – a club sandwich (one day he'll write an ode to The Club) – and after his sandwich he will see friends, this one and that one, and they'll be happy, three strangers in a city they've made their own. This is our city.

But this is yet to come.

The river is a series of __s. Lying down ls. The __ as place-holder for obscenity or to avoid naming a place, a time: the city, the street. On B__ Street in S__ in the year 20__. The man doesn't tell his friends that he's staying in a hotel ten minutes walk from here, that he is, for the weekend, a tourist in this city. While they ogle pretty boys and eat frozen yoghurt, his friends have no idea in what capacity he's inhabiting this city. As a writer, he works best as a tourist. He prefers to be passing through, to act as if his home is far from here, as if he has no permanency in this city. I'm just passing through, for a few days to sample what the city has to offer: art, men, ice cream.

Those of us who've transitioned into another tongue know that language is freedom, that moment when you're no longer functioning in a single language, the one that got you from a to b, that you transacted in, a language that in this new place, the place you've landed up in, a child denied the freedom to make your own choices and gradually, by osmosis, through learning, listening, observing, you acquired a new tongue and emerged from the transparency of a single language to navigate the world anew: talk to strangers, make love, moisten your palate.

That's you, a young man of sixteen, alone with strangers on the beach, following them into the dunes. You thought of it as making love, there in the dunes on your towel sucking cock, swallowing cum, jerking each other off, in the source language of the word onanism, a man who spilt (spilt, I said, not spit) his seed and by spilling gave his name to the activity we love so much, now even more so in a world full of stimulation.

We have never in all of history been so stimulated.

I'm positive, the man says.

I'm not, I say.

Let's get a room, he says.

But I don't know you, I say.

It's not like I'm going to murder you, he says.

Are you not? I say.

Come, he says.

But I'm scared. Can we talk? Can I stop being one, a thing walking alone, the I in the storm. Hold me. If we get a room, won't we slip into roles, top, bottom, no room for play.

Twenty years in this city and what have you got to show for it?

Who are you? I say.

In what way? he say.

In any way you want, I say.

Some men come to mind regularly. Joshua. Ahmed. Noel. Even Arturo. Mainly Joshua. Mainly Ahmed. I should rename them. I'll call you Stefan. No, Milan. I'll call you Mustafa, Saleh, Abdul. I'll call you Abdul, the name of a young man who lives in my block, still a teenager, still becoming; like him, your name is Abdul, full of the joy of becoming.

What happens to *un amour disparu*?

There you are on Facebook, your friend request still dangling in mid-air.

NO	ONE	
	ONE	DIRECTION
ANY	ONE	
SOME	ONE	
	ONE	LOVE
	ONE	TO ONE
ONE ON	ONE	
THE POWER OF	ONE	
AT	ONE	
AT	ONE	WITH
HOLE IN	ONE	
THE	ONE	

Take what you've been given and what you've gleaned (aren't they the same?) and sit before this rectangle as before a chalet window. This piece of paper is what matters, this page and how to fill it, cover me in words for I am sick with love. The ink takes up only a fraction (10%? less?), the rest is a white space around these letters that make up the words staccatoing across the page, west to east. Not all of us, and not me for a

13

while, when I wrote in that other language, no longer just one language, but a new one, a language lived in for a sizeable chunk, moving on the page from east to west, having moved out of Africa and into the frying pan of Palestine.

Safely ensconced in this city, I move again from left to right, the movement of pen on paper, moving towards the right, always towards the right, only to be taken back to the left; that's where every line begins. Sometimes a line is the beginning of a sentence but mainly it's the first sentence. Others start elsewhere, close to the eastern shores of the page.

Everywhere in the world the masses are moving towards the right.

The masses! And then there's me. Ass-s.

One-letter words
　a
　b, as in U b 2
　c, as in c u l8r
　e, repeated: eee! (I'm scared)
　I
　'k as in okay
　m, repeated mmm
　o, repeated ooo
　O as in of, Will O' (weep for me)
　p, as in a Number One (to rhyme with Three)

q, que? What did you say?

r as in r u ok?

s, repeated sss

U for the respectful Afrikaans you.

x as in my x

y as in y not?

z, repeated: zzz

The Hebrew for one: אחד. *Echad*. חד + א. The *aleph* plus the word for sharp, *chad*. To start the counting with the first letter of the alphabet, yes, that's nice, and then a word that means sharp but is also sharp, a harsh word, *chad*, straight from the back of the throat, clearing it to spit into each other's mouths.

Look at us making love.

The first is soft – *eh* – the blowing out of breath.

In English: One. First the blowing out of breath, *wwwhhh*, whispered, then the tongue rising to the palette to bring an end to that brief moment of surprise. *un*! Undone.

For the past few years, maybe five, maybe more, I've been writing in my notebooks in inks of different colours: pink, orange, purple, green, colourful pens a lover brought from Taiwan, pens he wrote in, and for a long time I wrote in, changing colours as I went through the pages of my Moleskine. Before that, I'd written with blue ballpoint pens in spiral-bound notepads. There was a time when I said I would never write in black, when I believed I would write in blue for the rest of my life. Anything else was unimaginable, and I didn't long for another possibility and at last there was some certainty in my life, something I'd chosen to do, for there's very little certainty in this life, not with the way I keep abandoning places and people until there is only one left and that one is me. The blue pen was my certainty and then after the blue pen – how could I have written only in blue? – my certainty was in a range of colours, gel pens from Japan bought by a Taiwanese lover, then later bought in bulk from an eBay seller in Hong Kong, and for years that was how I wrote, some days in purple, some in pink, some in orange.

"Psychopaths prefer green ink," a student told me.

Maybe that was the point when things started to change, I wasn't sure about writing in different colours, although at that time it was only green that bothered me. There was a dark yellow I stopped writing in and even orange didn't feel certain enough so I used it on rare occasions to add variety to the colours in my notebooks. How serious can one be in pink ink? Now I'm like: It's black or blue or nothing.

ONE DAY OF REST
ONE CITY
ONE ROOM

ONE GOD
ONE DAY I WILL
ONCE UPON A TIME

One is the first odd number, though not according to the Pythagoreans (the who?). For them, 1 is not a number because a number is plural and 1 is just itself. According to them, 1 is the source of all numbers. $1+1+1+1$, etc. One is the source, the first non-zero number, between nothing and together. One is the empty product. Any number multiplied by 1 is that number. But isn't 1 the *enabling* product, that which enables any number to be itself when multiplied by it. No other number can do that. In multiplication, one changes nothing. Something tells me a mathematician would tell me I'm talking shit.

One is noun, adjective, and pronoun. One = I and 1. One = you. One = a person. Do you want these ones? Thanks, but I'd rather have the red ones. All three numbers of my birth. 15. 12. 19__. I have always been a team of one, warding off others, scaring them off to be left alone, happiest on my own. Moments of bliss: those days on the farm in Bundanon walking down to the Shoalhaven, our secluded river bank, tranquil except for the occasional motorboat, or boys on the opposite bank swinging from the rope into the water. Late-morning, mid-afternoon swimming, melting into the landscape, water, trees, the

wide river (too scared to swim across, but Anna did).
Diving in and out of the water like a dolphin, along
the edge of the shore where the water starts to deepen,
propelling oneself up into the air, then diving back in.
Over and over. Look, that's me diving in and out of the
water, naked, my shorts on the banks of the river.

Back in the hotel room I stand before the mirror to take
a traditional selfie, like the ones on hook-up sites, men
with tops off in bathroom mirrors, locker-room mirrors,
hotel-room mirrors. In this selfie: An oblong face, A
double chin. Hair cropped close to the skull. Narrow
eyes, flared nostrils. Pale skin (uncreased). Brown-green
eyes. Hazel. A blue V-neck T-shirt to match the light
blue of the wall. The ears. Thin eyebrows. An Adam's
apple, a hint of stubble. A collarbone. I was beautiful
once. In pictures from 20, 30 years ago, I am beautiful.
Now I'm not. It's not always like this, not all pictures
of me are ugly, but in this one I am ugly. This could be
the face of a criminal. This is the picture they'll show
if I'm arrested for something newsworthy, the face of a
recluse, hiding from direct sunlight and joy. This is what
the city does to one, what happens when you stay put for
too long, when you keep knocking on the wrong doors,
eat too much, fuck too much because you've given up
on love.

In the self portrait you're looking at, the man's head

is shaved, his scalp shining in the light, yellow. There are shades of pink and orange in his jaundiced look. The nostrils are deep, the eyes narrow slits in yellow-green caverns. The lips are thin and pale, almost the same colour as his flesh. The man lifts his head to the viewer. How can you know that this is the face of a man who has just made love, the face of a man who spent the evening with friends eating frozen yoghurt, the face of a man who has come back to his room, a room with pale blue walls and a window looking out onto The Shard, train tracks going in and out of London Bridge Station. He can still taste the coffee, the sweet cold yoghurt, still hear the conversation with the stranger.

This is the room in which I write.

I have: apples, a bag of muesli, a pint of milk (it will curdle overnight in this room with no mini-bar), a slab of chocolate, 72%. By the bedside: remote control and ear plugs. Clean white linen on the bed. A duvet. Four pillows.

This is a room for more than one person.

I have come to this room to write. It seems like this, a room like this, is the one place I can gather my thoughts, gather words, let go into them. There are no choices to make in a room like this. For too long I have been outside words, unable to write, unwilling. I'm here to find something to say, to find a way to stop repeating myself, to write something different, something to re-enter the world with. As if repetition is the greatest crime, to keep repeating oneself. Oneself: repeated. The true artist is the exception. Malevich is the exception. Matisse – the exception. Kandinsky. *He* is not the exception. Meaning, I'm not. Someone like Malevich, changing, moving from style to style, could it be they didn't know what to say, that this constant search for ways to say creates an illusion of progression.

At Tate Modern this afternoon (but I thought we were on the banks of the Shoalhaven) re-visiting the Malevich exhibition, a thrilling surprise when my mother had been here last week and suggested we see it. Not just Matisse, but Malevich, too. There he is in the first room, self-portrait in green, blue and red.

In the middle room, a guy in a yarmulke. I want to go up to him, make a joke about seeing art on *shabbes*, that money must have changed hands, and I think of my mother who'd been in France a few weeks ago and seeing a man with a yarmulke on the Metro had wanted to go up to him and kiss him. I said nothing because the story echoed what had happened to me a couple of days before at the gym when a guy a few lockers down from me got dressed, clipped on his yarmulke and left the changing room, and I'd wanted to run after him and say: I am your people.

Blue is the colour of Malevich's hair, eyebrows, narrow sideburns. Red shirt, black bow tie, not a bow tie exactly, one of those butterfly things, white collar with embroidery at the tip of each flap, a sickle on the left. Turquoise and green jacket, a deep-sea blue, bottomless lakes. Light divides his face, the shadow half in shades of green, the other side – yellow. Young enough for his frown not to crease his brow. The bright blue of his gaze fixed on us, on himself, the painter.

What is the point of sitting alone in a room with a notebook, a black pen, coffee, a desk, a mirror, a bottle of water, a kettle and a mug and a pint of milk that will sour, a pair of glasses that are not my reading glasses because my reading glasses are on my nose as I write the story of my weekend: Woke at 08:17, made coffee, ate blueberries, peed, drank coffee, listened to the Today programme with John Humphries and Sue McGregor (but she's been gone for years). Pour muesli from a blue Alpen bag into a pale blue bowl, add milk and listen to the story of the 1,400 girls groomed and raped and abused by men in Rotherham. A woman who'd been involved in the investigations said she'd left to take care of her dying husband and when she came back to work, nothing had been done, despite all the leads, despite the girls' statements, despite the work she'd done to find several girls willing to talk. Even after they persuaded her to investigate similar crimes, she witnessed the inaction of the authorities, their fear of being labelled racist.

Is that really why they hushed up the evidence, why they ignored the stories the girls told? And the parents? Teachers and friends and parents of friends who knew stuff was happening and said nothing? Isn't the real question or one of the questions: who are we as a society, who are these people, these English people, who are they as a society when they let something like this happen? This story that gets repeated of the insignificance of the lives of certain types of people.

| + | + | + | + | + | + | + | + | + | + | + | + | + | + | + | + | + | + | +
| + | + | + | + | + | + | + | + | + | + | + | + | + | + | + | + | + | + | +
| + | + | + | + | + | + | + | + | + | + | + | + | + | + | + | + | + | + | +
| + | + | + | + | + | + | + | + | + | + | + | + | + | + | + | + | + | + | +
| + | + | + | + | + | + | + | + | + | + | + | + | + | + | + | + | + | + | +
| + | + | + | + | + | + | + | + | + | + | + | + | + | + | + | + | + | + | +
| + | + | + | + | + | + | + | + | + | + | + | + | + | + | + | + | + | + | +
| + | + | + | + | + | + | + | + | + | + | + | + | + | + | + | + | + | + | +
| + | + | + | + | + | + | + | + | + | + | + | + | + | + | + | + | + | + | +
| + | + | + | + | + | + | + | + | + | + | + | + | + | + | + | + | + | + | +
| + | + | + | + | + | + | + | + | + | + | + | .+ | + | + | + | + | + | + | +
| + | + | + | + | + | + | + | + | + | + | + | + | + | + | + | + | + | + | +
| + | + | + | + | + | + | + | + | + | + | + | + | + | + | + | + | + | + | +
| + | + | + | + | + | + | + | + | + | + | + | + | + | + | + | + | + | + | +
| + | + | + | + | + | + | + | + | + | + | + | + | + | + | + | + | + | + | +
| + | + | + | + | + | + | + | + | + | + | + | + | + | + | + | + | + | + | +
| + | + | + | + | + | + | + | + | + | + | + | + | + | + | + | + | + | + | +

| + | + | + | + | + | + | + | + | + | + | + | + | + | + | + | + | + | +
| + | + | + | + | + | + | + | + | + | + | + | + | + | + | + | + | + | +
| + | + | + | + | + | + | + | + | + | + | + | + | + | + | + | + | + | +
| + | + | + | + | + | + | + | + | + | + | + | + | + | + | + | + | + | +
| + | + | + | + | + | + | + | + | + | + | + | + | + | + | + | + | + | +
| + | + | + | + | + | + | + | + | + | + | + | + | + | + | + | + | + | +
| + | + | + | + | + | + | + | + | + | + | + | + | + | + | + | + | + | +
| + | + | + | + | + | + | + | + | + | + | + | + | + | + | + | + | + | +
| + | + | + | + | + | + | + | + | + | + | + | + | + | + | + | + | + | +
| + | + | + | + | + | + | + | + | + | + | + | + | + | + | + | + | + | +
| + | + | + | + | + | + | + | + | + | + | + | + | + | + | + | + | + | +
| + | + | + | + | + | + | + | + | + | + | + | + | + | + | + | + | + | +
| + | + | + | + | + | + | + | + | + | + | + | + | + | + | + | + | + | +
| + | + | + | + | + | + | + | + | + | + | + | + | + | + | + | + | + | +
| + | + | + | + | + | + | + | + | + | + | + | + | + | + | + | + | + | +
| + | + | + | + | + | + | + | + | + | + | + | + | + | + | + | + | + | +
| + | + | + | + | + | + | + | + | + | + | + | + | + | + | + | + | + | +
| + | + | + | + | + | + | + | + | + | + | + | + | + | + | + | + | + | +
| + | + | + | + | + | + | + | + | + | + | + | + | + | + | + | + | + | +
| + | + | + | + | + | + | + | + | + | + | + | + | + | + | + | + | + | +
| + | + | + | + | + | + | + | + | + | + | + | + | + | + | + | + | + | +
| + | + | + | + | + | + | + | + | + | + | + | + | + | + | + | + | + | +
| + | + | + | + | + | + | + | + | + | + | + | + | + | + | + | + | + | +
| + | + | + | + | + | + | + | + | + | + | + | + | + | + | + | + | + | +
| + | + | + | + | + | + | + | + | + | + | + | + | + | + | + | + | + | +
| + | + | + | + | + | + | + | + | + | + | + | + | + | + | + | + | + | +
| + | + | + | + | + | + | + | + | + | + | + | + | + | + | + | + | + | +
| + | + | + | + | + | + | + | + | + | +

And that's only half the girls abused, each one a child damaged, finding a way to heal, fighting the urge to believe in their worthlessness, a child – now an adult, many of them adults – with as much chance to survive as to finish off what the adults started.

I is the accusing finger, pointing to ask: Will you always write about smut, about the goings on in the places you go to. I is the censoring finger, the voice to shut you up, stop you from talking about who you are, who your people are. What if the accusing I is me, is my finger pointing at my people asking them what the fuck are we doing.

In this subterranean place we are men looking for sex.

One steam room and another steam room, a dry sauna, a large one, another smaller one at the foot of the stairs. We walk the corridors for sex. Some of us – me, for example – want love. That's me in a white towel cruising the corridors, me in the dry sauna with a stranger on his knees, my cock pushing against the back of his throat, me on the top bench with the man who has come up for air, two fingers in his mouth pushing deeper, past his throat to feel the beginning of his oesophagus. That's me holding the back of his head as I push my fingers deep into his throat, my mouth close to his whispering that's it, that's it. Men gather to watch, one stands close, side by side with the man I am kissing.

Later, we will do more in the cabin upstairs.

Later, back in the dry sauna, I will speak to the tall Uighur guy whose name in Uighur is a common name for a girl in Hebrew. He tells me he's from China but that he doesn't speak Chinese. He tells me he's from a small group of people with a very ancient history. He has a strong Russian accent and a sardonic – is that the word I'm looking for? – sense of humour. Do you live in London? I ask, and his answer is something like: I was floating in the sky for many days and eventually landed in this place, gesturing to the sauna in which we are both sitting.

That's very precise, I say.

Right into your arms, he says.

So I move closer. I don't remember exactly what we said to each other, but it was playful, and he had that Russian demeanour that feels familiar to me, a sense of humour I like, not a flabby sense of humour, not the English sense of humour borne out of frustration and repression and a terror of the body and fucking. None of that. His was gutsy, aggressive. Was he flirting with me or making fun of me, joking, fooling around? I looked for him later in the corridors upstairs, hoped he'd reappear when I was back in the dry sauna, but I never found him again. Instead I hooked up with a Filipino guy I'd hooked up with before, a guy who kept telling me I was perfect, a guy who was visibly turned on by me, liked everything about me. But there was no chemistry, and there was a moment when we were lying in the cubicle and the porn was playing on the screen in that small room and I felt like this was the moment in the movie when the main character is depicted at his lowest point, the moment he realises we are all doomed, and the soundtrack is something like Bach or Elgar, and the scene as ruthless as that moment in *Apocalypse Now* when the fighting is going on and some symphony is playing.

I is the phallus.

That moment when the main character is in a situation that he doesn't want to be in, doing things he doesn't want to do, and you see a sadness in his expression, the weight of it, and on the screen in the cubicle where the main character is lying naked with the Filipino guy, two porn stars, one of them with tattoos across his chest and the other teasing his arsehole with his fingers, and the camera zooms in, and George, the Filipino guy, says to me, next time we'll do that, but I want you to shave your arsehole, but my arsehole is shaved, feel, it's shaved. It's all so depressing and the critics are saying: Why does he have to show all the negative sides of being gay, that's not how most of us live our lives, not a reality we recognise. Why, in this day and age, do we have to keep telling the same sordid story, that story we saw on the screens in the 80s in *Cruising* and whatever other films they were making back then, *The Boys in the Band*, portraying us in such a negative light, so negative! and now we must see it again.

Not again, the critic says.

That's me with the accusing finger.

It's at this moment that the main character decides to change his life. From this moment on, everything will change. It's uplifting. It's a feel-good movie that people – the gays – will watch over and over because it will reflect their lives and offer them hope, even if they don't plan to do anything to change who they are, they will have glimpsed the possibility and will know that at some point they, too, can shift into something better.

Today is the Sabbath. The day of rest. God, too, got tired. Six days and enough already. Give. Me. A break. On the seventh day God put his feet up. But in the beginning. This is where it all begins. The one. One, our God our God our God, who exists in heaven and on earth. This is what we sing at the end of the *seder*, a song that gets louder and louder as you progress, until we're all shouting "Our God, Our God, who's in the sky and on the ground," working off a vast meal we've been force fed, matzo balls weighing us down.

The upright digit, the 1 is the crack in the door. Pry it open to see inside. A room with blue carpets and three white walls, one wall is blue, and the pictures of a blue something on the wall behind the bed, and the red dot –

is it just one dot? – sold to the man in the blue whatever. The room. The room in which he writes.

Sunday

I don't know where I'm going but when you're with me, I'm okay. We'd walked that long walk (which you hated) from the West End back to Finsbury Park. You hate everything about the city, or at least that's what you say, but like so many of us you're stuck here, dependant on its money and its untiring supply of men. Few cities in the world can provide as many men in as many different varieties as this city. That's what keeps us here. The hope of a boyfriend, a husband, someone to be with so we don't have to be alone with these obsessions that keep us awake at night.

I wasn't giving enough. You wanted more.

We liked walking. For you, it was a calling, a need, to walk alone. You've never found anyone who likes to walk the way you do, slowly and over wide expanses. Just you and your backpack, 20 kilos to your body weight of 60, treading across the Sierra Nevada, across Dartmoor, across Lapland in summer with the snow still on the ground. You and your backpack, some food, some clothes, a tent. I love that about you, the way you traverse great distances on foot, planning, researching, weighing the food, each portion of oatmeal in its own zip-lock bag.

Walk faster.

On another walk, this time from Finsbury Park to Highgate, I'm looking for a fight. You aren't giving me enough and I want more. More care, more interest in my story. Ask me questions, interrogate my, open your eyes wide when I begin to recount the story of my day. Two men battling for attention, and the less you give me, the more I withhold. I prefer the company of strangers. Any coupling will do, as long as I feel loved. I'm the baby bird going from creature to creature, asking: Are you my mother?

If One is the Father, Two is the Mother. The Child comes next.

Two is the creative force. Two is now. If one was the past, yesterday, two is today, now, this. Two is the earth, far from the airy fairy nonsense of the heavens, the made-up stories of the past, clinging to memory. Memory is only good for the making up of stories. What does it serve in the present, in the now, today? Two is today, this. Two is this. The propelling of words across the page, but really, just running on the spot when you're on a keyboard, a kind of rambling, rumbling, staccato dashing from letter to letter, so many Ts, your fingers coming back to the tea, the T. The coffee. Freshly brewed. Your second cup to make the present easier, to make staying awake on this earth easier, to make the tap-tapping of your fingers on the keyboard, your eyes on your fingers – look away from the screen – as you watch your fingers, not all of them, you're not using all of them but you do use two hands but only three fingers of the one hand and your index finger of the other, but it is two hands, you wouldn't be able to do it this quick with one hand, and your fingers feel nimble, yes, once you were nibble, I mean, nimble, oh, there we go, the past jumping in, another sob story to tell or a happy memory from your agile days, when you ran into the water, dashed into the sea, danced until four in the morning then walked from Jaffa to North Tel Aviv, stopping off to swim with L and Y, the three of you naked, or was it just you, the lights from the promenade and the restaurants that stay open all night illuminating the sand and the moon which is always in the sky and the sky is always clear, shining its light onto you. Oh my, how nimble you were and the men, some men, mainly ones you weren't interested in, fell in love with you. You've always been the type who falls in love with men who are not interested in you. It goes back. The horror of the past that lingers, nagging to be repeated because that's what it knows, that's the story imprinted on your soul and your soul feels more comfortable when it's drowning in torment and the deep sense of rejection. What's that kind of love called?

Unrequited makes you nimble.

Two is the Soul. If one is the Body, two is the Soul.

Two are the animals, the tablets of the Ten Commandments. 1) Be nice. 2) Be nice to your mom and dad. 3) Don't kill people. 4) Be nice to your aunties and neighbours. 5) Don't sleep with people in your family. That sort of thing. And be nice to The One who is God in the heavens and on the earth.

In the dream I'd killed someone. I killed him for you, the fat girl at school. I had smashed him to death and then burnt the straw that was left of his body. And the torment, my God, the torment that came after that. In the dream I remember thinking that it wasn't the guilt of killing someone – he deserved to die, or he was unloved, inconsequential, he had no family, nobody missed him – but what really tormented me in the dream was the desire to confess, to tell the story, and I remember thinking that if I could just tell the story, confess to having killed him, then everything would be fine. And there was the fear that she would tell, that I had to keep her sweet so she wouldn't tell anyone. In the minutes of waking up, hovering between sleep and light, I doubted whether I'd been dreaming or if this was real, if I had really killed someone, and I went through various ways of checking, asking myself if I had actually done it.

To kill is to always be connected. It's like borrowing or lending money, except in this case it's a life, a life, like a loan that can never be returned, an uncuttable umbilical between you and the other person. If you kill me, I am yours forever. I don't need to light a candle every year to remember you, that candle burns for you always.

Last night I could have killed him, could have ripped out his throat when he gave himself to me. The Spaniard gave himself to me. No names. And he's like: I wish I had poppers so I could go deeper with you and I'm like that was pretty deep and he's like no, I want deeper. Men who give themselves to you, just like that, lambs to the slaughter, another one of us whose life means nothing. It's a glorious feeling to feel like nothing, to have no body, no will, no future, all there is is now and the letting go into nothingness. The bright future is the stark shining light of death.

Two is yes and no. One says yes and the other says no. Two is good and evil. Two is too and to. Two is me and the other guy. Being and nothingness, left and right, east west, north south, together alone. It's night and day. What did you say? We're like chalk and cheese. More cheese please, Louise, she calls from the dinner table in the kitchen at lunchtime when the kids rush in for food. More cheese please, Louise. Two is birth and death. Two is right and wrong, true and false, yin yang, positive negative.

I'm positive, he said.

I'm negative, I said.

So we did it, me making my way into him, surrendering to whatever may come, and for those moments two became one. Two bodies in one soul, or the other way round, or one body in another body equals what? For those brief moments we were in love, were we not?

Two is conflict. It takes two to. Two to tango, two to fuck. More is good, but all you need for a good fight, a good fuck, a good waltz is two. With tango, only two can work. Two is two-faced, the duplicitous English.

Two is twins. Two is joy. One for sorrow. Three for a girl.

2 is the swan. 2 is the breast, the pregnant belly.

Two is judgement and balance, the scales, this side and that, the woman coming in from market weighed down by baskets. Two is duality and duplicity. Two is hard to understand, hard to make out. Two is the binary to make things easy. But the word is neither this nor that, either or, one or the other. Two is just a number on the spectrum. We are all, all of us, every single one of us, somewhere else on the spectrum, either at one end or the other and the million points in between.

Two is together, a partnership, me and you, moving between harmony and rivalry. Two brothers and two sisters, too. You can choose, this one or that. Two makes it easier to pick one. I choose you.

Two is the Son because three is the Holy Spirit. The ghost. Two is life, as in birth then life then death. Two is either male or female, but I told you it's a spectrum, we're all on the spectrum... don't say male/female. Let's get rid of that. Yes, but the homosexuals like to say: He's so masculine. You're a real man. I like my men to be men. Me, I tell you, I like my men to be faggots. I like my men to be like you, skinny and pliable, so open that all you need is a bit of spit.

Two is the sabbath candles lit by the lady of the house, open palms circling the flames, gathering in the glow, covering eyes to say the *brocha*. The man blesses the bread and wine, the blood and body of Christ eaten in chunks, washed down with wine from a silver goblet, passed round the table every Friday night in the Jewish households of the world. *L'chaim* and *amen*. And what were *you* doing on *Shabbes* night?

Two's ruling planet is the moon, whatever that means, to keep us company at night, lighting the way when we run into the water after dancing till 4am. That's what the moon does, waxes and wanes. You're either waxing or waning, whatever that means. Excuse me, are you a waxer or a waner. (Note to self: Look up the meaning of waxing and waning in the context of the moon.) If One is Unity then Two is Duality. The opposition, separation, antagonism. He taught me to fight. All my life I've lived in terror of a fight, avoided fights, pushed my body to become the kind of body that would help me keep out of fights. Mind the way you walk, mind your voice, the way you stand, avoid eye contact. George changed all that, he taught me how to punch, left hook, right hook, jab, kick, upper cut. George is responsible for the waning of my fear.

Two is the charitable relationship, to give and receive. I'm more comfortable on the giving end. Receiving makes me feel small and I don't like to feel small. I don't trust that you'll love me after you've seen me so small, receiving with my legs in the air, on all fours with my arse facing outwards. Please come in, make yourself at home. I would give myself to George. On some level, I'm infatuated with George. The other day, George stroked my head. George this, George that. George, I say, and I say this in the dream, do you love me?

The problem is that I've spent very little of my life in a two, a few weeks here, a few months there, not much more than that. Add up the time I've spent as two, and you might get 5 years max. Ten percent of my life has been spent in two, as a couple, one of a pair. If I hooked up with someone right now and lived to 100, I'll have spent more than half my life as a couple. I know people, and I'm thinking of one in particular whose name begins with G (not George) who has lived most of his life, from 18 to 54, in a couple. Two-thirds of his life, probably more, in a couple, one of two, as a pair, in and out of each other's bodies. Not that he's happy, not that he's found the one, but it's what he does, it's how he lives. On the whole, he's a fairly miserable human being. Being one of two is not about happiness, it's about creation, bringing things into the world, coming up with ways to forget you are one. Being two is about forgetting. As a one, so much of what you grapple with is the past. Some people who live as a two bring babies into the world, others find the strength to create more meaningful stuff. Art, for example. Charity, for example.

Two is the middle. Piggy in the.

TWO FACED

TWO TO TANGO

IT TAKES TWO

Two is the duel, the dual. I'm going for a Number Two, and off he trots to the loo. He has the trots. Hey sonny boy, where you off to, Number One or Two? (Though it should be Number Two or Three?) My fingers keep getting confused and writing Tow instead of Two. Two is Tow, the pulling of one by the other, towing the car, towing the ship or person or whatever it is that needs to be towed to safety. And if Tow then why not Toe? Two is the parts of the body: eyes, nostrils, ears, cheeks, lips, nipples, armpits, shoulders, arms, rib cages, balls, legs, thighs, feet, fallopian tubes. Multiples of two are neater. If you have eleven toes, that's a problem. But is it? Is it a balance issue? Two is balance. Two is the second, and on the second day God created. Note to self: Check what he created then. Heaven and earth?

Today is Sunday, the day of rest and prayer for our

Christian brethren. Can you hear that? In the distance, the bells of Southwark Cathedral, or the bells of St Paul's, or both? The bells of two cathedrals competing: Come and pray with us.

I'm running out of things 2 say.

Two is the diptych, the man and his wife, the burgher and his frau, the patron and his partner. Two is side by side, two is one plus one, two is together. And when God decided that it was all a big mistake and he'd start from scratch, or from more-or-less scratch, he made Noah, played by Bruce Willis, no, the Australian actor, what's his name, to build an arc and take in two by twos: armadillos, baboons, crocodiles, deer, elephants, finches, goats, etc etc. Can you imagine the lot of them in a boat rocking hither and thither on the high seas all because God wasn't happy with his first draft.

Let's start again, only this time I have more of a plan. Well, not really a plan, but this might work. Let's try it this way. Let's focus on the animals. Let's start with a single family, mom, dad, a few kids, all ready to go. All aboard and off we go. The rest of you drown. There's room for the animals, but for you – not so much. No room for you, or you, or you, or you, or you, or you. | + | + | + | all over again. Do you have any idea how many people that is, how many people got left behind all because God decides it's Noah and his *mishpuchah* and two each of the two-by-twos who get to be there when the new dawn breaks.

In the dream you are without arms and legs and your head
has been lobbed off. A thick fleshy torso, leaning to the
right, stretching the left side of your body. You balance
on stumps, your buttocks fleshy, your love handles
plump. And your lovers: stacks of phalluses disguised
as bananas. In the name of decency, you turn bulbuls
into ripe bananas. This is what remains of your lovers. I
retitle you: The Artist and His Lovers. In the dream, you
think to yourself: Is the banana always a penis? Or is it
home? Do bananas in the now stand for batches of them
ripening in the garage of the house on Jenvey Road. The
artist and his home. Call it that. In the distance the train,
city hall, the suspension bridge. The train in the distance
there to illustrate that the poet left home long ago. But
wasn't it on a train that he first made love to a Gentile,
him a boy of 13 and the soldier heading for the border up
north, to fight, to kill, perchance to die.

I like it when you sit in the background. Me the artist in
my see-through blouse, fleshy nipples and strands of chest
hair showing, and you behind me, nipples erect, your face
scarred – it was me who took the knife to your cheek – to
ward off other men. Ha, try that with the homosexuals!
That's not going to work. They love danger and scars
and evidence of near-death experiences. You're mine,
scarred by my ownership. Narcissus blooms from behind
your left shoulder.

We're approaching the end, been like this for far too long, grumpy, unsatisfied, tainted by my whatever. I like it when you recline naked on the sofa, the checkered blanket, the striped pillows, the crumpled white sheet. I like it when you're tense, afraid, on edge: that's when I know you're mine, when I've got you where I want you. That's the kind of guy I am when I'm one of two. Last night's dream intrudes. Did I kill him, did I really kill him, would it help to confess? I will do anything not to be 2. And in the real background: the city. In the real background: the night. Beyond you: the city at night, that time when we are most naked, no longer anticipating errand or interruption. Come quick, he's dying. We prepare for bed, for fucking, for the sweet release of self-centred sleep.

Monday

Three for a girl. Three is we. Three little piggies, wee wee wee. Three wes (we we we). I like threesomes with couples. Me and a we. Three is the end, beginning middle and. Three is the Holy Spirit. The Power of Three. Three is the son, product of mom and dad. Three cheers. Hip hip hooray. I don't like endings, though I do like Mondays. I'm good at beginnings, starting stuff, getting excited about you, an idea, but then things fizzle out, I lose interest, ready for the next episode of enthusiasm. I'm promiscuous in everything. It's a Sag thing. Once is great, twice is great, but I'm bored by the time we get to three. Birth is nice, life is nice, but what then?

In my room like all rooms in this chain of hotels, there is: a bed, hangers, a desk, a mirror (one above the desk, one by the door, one in the bathroom). The bathroom is in the bedroom, a shape in the corner of the bedroom, a square within a square, but in the bathroom's case, with the edge sliced off like a dog-end? And so in this room of squares and rectangles – or maybe everything is a rectangle – the bed, the bathroom. The room is 21 steps long, from door to window, and 12 steps wide. The bed is 6 and a half by 6 steps. The outer walls of the bathroom, if the snipped off bit where the door is wasn't there, is 9 steps by 9 steps. The desk is 9 and a half steps long and just under 3 steps wide. My feet are a size 45 in Europe, just to give us all a sense of how big a step is.

The bath tiles, or fake bath tiles, because everything in the bathroom is plastic, the bath tiles are a deep red. But that's not true, the tiles are real tiles, from bath-tub to ceiling and on the wall behind the sink and toilet, a deep red. Crimson tiles with white grouting. The red is mirrored in the round disk on the print above the bed, a kind of bauble in a very close up image of glitter. This could be a blurry close up of one of those fake Christmas trees, shimmering white, a pale blue on one side and gradually moving towards navy on the other. The red bauble is closer to the top right-hand corner. I am looking at the print in the mirror above the desk so I have to turn to check what side the bauble is on. In the mirror it's in the top left-hand corner.

The window looks out onto a shape that stabs itself into the sky. No, that's not what I want to say. It is a triangle of crystal rising from the ground. The city has a spike, a splinter, a shard of glass.

Eventually – but this is in the future (past, present, and) – the man (me) will leave London, leave this city that has been his for more than twenty years, and move to another city, another language. For now, he lies on his bed in his room in this hotel. He has had his breakfast, has made himself a second mug of coffee. Soon he will pack his few belongings that he brought with him for the weekend and check out of the hotel. He will get on his bike and cycle the thirty minutes back to his flat in the north east of the city and sit at his desk with a fresh cup of coffee and type up these notes, these notes from the weekend, his weekend, the weekend that was his and which he spent in that hotel in that city that is no longer his.

Two Doors Down

Long after we left that street and that city and the country we'd lived in, we talked about the family from two doors down. At family dinners we'd speak about the neighbourhood: remember this? remember that? – and most things we did remember, but when it came to that family we didn't remember much: not their names, except for the girl, Deirdre, who was my sister's age, nor could we agree on exactly how many siblings there were. Some of us said four and some thought six: there was an older sister, older than the oldest brother, who was older than Deirdre, and perhaps there'd been a younger sister, maybe a baby, younger than the youngest brother, the boy who'd been kicked in the teeth by a horse.

Our house was the last on Jenvey Road, a street like most others in Summerstrand, the newest of the neighbourhoods in Port Elizabeth. Next to us, moving towards Brewer Road, was an empty lot, although when I visited a few years ago, a couple of houses had been built there, houses with high walls from behind which you could hear dogs barking, though they could have been the Alsatians in the garden of the house we used to live in, the house our father built.

When I say built, I don't mean built built, because we're not that kind of family, not in the way some families have men who put up shelves or lay bricks. We were like the other Jewish families: the Rummels, the Ryans, the Schewitzes, and our cousins who lived on Admiralty Way. During the week, our fathers were shopkeepers, doctors, or chemists. Our mothers, on the whole, did not work. The family from two doors down was the only non-Jewish family I knew back then, and for a long time after that, too. They had a swimming pool, the only house on Jenvey Road that had one. There were paving stones around it and glass doors on all sides, so that the pool area was like a conservatory with aloe plants and bougainvillea. We had a lawn big enough for a jungle gym, a vegetable patch, hoopoo birds gathered on the grass in the mornings. Years later, the new people who bought the house built a pool in the garden and a granny shack in which a granny lived until she died. When I visited, long after we'd left the country, more than twenty years later, the granny shack was being used as a guest house.

"Come stay whenever you like," the new people said, and although I said I would, I knew I'd never go back to that city, and maybe never to that country either.

If I went back, I might try and find out what happened to Deirdre and her family. They may have been Afrikaners, poor, darker than us. They were wilder than anyone we knew, wild because the parents were never home, though I wouldn't be surprised, the way memory works, if I had actually met the parents. Maybe their wildness had something to do with them not having servants, as if they could fend for themselves. After all, the oldest of them must have been at least sixteen.

I couldn't have been more than ten, and if I was ten, then my older sister, and Deirdre, were fifteen, and if the brother was older, then he was at least sixteen and old enough to be in charge, although back then you didn't have to be that old to be in charge. We spent most of our time out of the house, roaming the streets, and when we were given bikes we dreamt of escape. We played at other people's houses, the Solomonses, the Friedmans, and in the pool of the family from two doors down.

All this happened somewhere between the late 1960s and early 1970s in apartheid South Africa, before we moved to the big house and eventually away from that town and that country.

The brother who'd been kicked by a horse had brown stubs for teeth that you could see when he spoke or smiled. Maybe they were just his baby teeth waiting to fall out, and the story about the horse was just a glib comment, a joke made by an older sibling, which we'd bought the way we bought other lies, throw-away remarks accepted as truth. A boy of six or seven, maybe eight, would not survive a kick in the teeth by a horse, and his brown teeth could have been the result of too much sugar and bad dental hygiene.

Some things will never be known. Memory is a flash of a moment, afternoons in a neighbour's pool, dive-bombing, racing each other, games played in other people's living rooms. Some memories are a single event spread out to cover an entire summer or the vast expanse of childhood. So we must be satisfied with this, the sweetness and abandon of what is remembered, the mystery of what cannot be retrieved.

"They had to move," my sister said recently. "They didn't live there very long, just that one summer. Someone told the police about them."

But even that isn't true. Even that isn't what happened during those brutal times in our country's history.

"I was asking around," my sister said. "Stuff you wouldn't believe."

They'd left the country, there were rumours the parents had gone to jail and the kids shipped off to live with relatives in the Karoo. One person said the older sister had been sent to London to have an abortion.

When we left that country we became like them, wild, slightly unhinged, smoking, drinking, skipping school, mornings on the beach, sleeping over at friends. We became the children parents didn't want their kids associating with. Our mother and father owned a shop in the centre of the town, a smaller shop than the one they'd had back home. The town was smaller, too, in a country far from where we were born. After school we'd help out in the shop, selling ornamental candles and decorative cushions. My mother reminded us recently about the week they'd closed the shop and how we'd stood outside and let people in, two at a time, to avoid overcrowding. People queued up to buy the last of the remaining stock.

I remember a room in that house two doors down. A bed. A single bed against a wall and me on the bed. We're playing a game after our swim – Ludo or Monopoly, maybe Snap – we're looking at comics, *Dagwood and Blondie, Casper, Richie Rich*. There's something sexual in the air, a kind of haze in that room, that house, as if they didn't want us to see what went on in the other rooms, how many of them slept together, shared a bed. We think the two boys shared, the brother who was eight and the brother who was sixteen. Maybe there was no reason to go anywhere else but the pool, the pool was why we were there. Maybe I don't remember what I saw. Maybe I saw and I don't remember. Maybe in the midst of a childhood of bullies and choosing sides for rugby teams, this was a happy moment, this was a time worth remembering. Maybe the narrative of a miserable childhood shovels everything into its maw. Maybe the family from two doors down were our refuge.

And then it was time to go home.

We'd had enough or it was dinner-time, our mother called us or their mother said it was time to go, or Agnes came to fetch us, or our sister stepped out of Deirdre's room and stood in the doorway of the boys' room and said: "We're going." So we walked up the road, past the Bernstein's house that separated us from the house two doors down and through the double garage doors where our mother's car was parked and maybe not yet our father's, who was still on his way home from work, and we made our way to wash up and wait for him to return so we could all sit down to dinner.

I Will Tell This Story

It's a puzzle to me, considering where I come from, how I got to be where I am now, in London living as a writer, getting books published, knowing all sorts of poets and publishers, some in real life, some through letters, some, admittedly, through Facebook, all of us recognizable to each other, even if just in pictures. Sometimes I think: What takes a shy, bullied (but wilful) boy from a small town on the tip of Africa and flings him across the continent, to the Levant, then later across Europe, thwacked like some dodgem car along the up and down sides of a triangle, propelled by the caprice of history and a momentum gained by centuries of pogroms and wickedness, to land up writing on a damp island amongst the offspring and survivors of the twisted and vicious English.

And then to make a career out of writing about the homosexuals, to be a queer Jew immigrant small-town writer-in-exile sustained, on the whole, by a community of dead writers, none of whom, as far as I know – and I know – cared about England or its Literature.

I was brought up in a part of the world remote enough for the Europeans to feel they were free to raid its land and debase its people. To a large extent these practices continue today, although the country is still remote enough for the Europeans to avoid being troubled by its neglect. My people came to Africa at the end of the nineteenth century, penniless, ignorant of the land they'd been enticed to. We escaped Lithuania, victims of an age-old hatred that is still fresh and vibrant in many parts of the world. Sometimes the only way to deal with misery is to leave.

My strongest memory of growing up in Port Elizabeth is a desire to get out, a feeling that there must be somewhere better. Perhaps that is a common desire amongst queer people – amongst all writers – especially those of us who have grown up in the small towns of the world. By the time I was fifteen, my family was packing its bags and getting ready to move to the Promised Land, a place in which we arrived not exactly penniless (no white person leaves South Africa penniless) but definitely ignorant. We moved to Ashkelon, a town even smaller than the one I was born in, a place to re-invent myself, and a new language to hide in.

The countries that have made me are immoral and damaged. But maybe the world is like that. And writing – art in general – is the antidote. How did I find my way into writing? Who were the writers who made me? I might have discovered Jack Kerouac through a young couple I babysat for while I was still in high-school, just before I went into the army. I think they had a copy of *Howl* on the bookshelf in their bedroom, maybe even on the same shelf as *Sensual Massage for Couples* which I leafed through and masturbated to while their baby slept.

The summer after the summer I discovered Kerouac, I went into the army. For the month of my basic training I carried *On the Road* with me, sometimes in my pocket. We were at war in Lebanon, and although not a combatant, I was sent to the front. I can't remember what I read during those years, and maybe when one starts to have sex in earnest, reading falls by the wayside. Sex and war are a lot to deal with, and I have spent most of my writing life trying to make sense of both.

Who taught me to write about sex? And by sex I mean desire and also the things we do with our bodies when we are naked in the company of another body. I mean the way we watch each other and touch. Where do we find the words and the ways to write about this? The impetus, the permission. Where do we find our writing ancestors? They find us. Our teachers? They find us. When the student is ready, the master and all that. *High Risk: An Anthology of Forbidden Writings* came to me from somewhere, and with it came John Preston. By the time I encountered Preston's work I was out of the army and writing short stories in Hebrew, taking my first steps as a journalist. I gave myself a Hebrew name. My transformation into a thing I was not was complete. I thought I could get away from me, away from the bullied small-town girl/boy moffie.

But in the *High Risk* anthology Dennis Cooper said I didn't have to, that I could say what I wanted and still not be as outrageous as him. Essex Hemphill said: Say it. David Wojnarowicz said that nothing was too filthy, no thought too shameful. But most of all it was John Preston who told me all I had to do was fuck and write. If I wrote frankly and openly about fucking, I'd be fine. I could make a career out of that.

I read *Mr Benson* and *I Once Had a Master* and other stories and essays by Preston. I wanted to live like him, to have my days filled with desire, to have a master, a brutal and caring lover like Pedro. I wanted to write like him. But in order to do that, I had to go back to English. To write with depth and precision about lust and the flesh, we must revert to our native tongues. The decision to stop writing in Hebrew and to return to the language I was born in was like diving into cool water. I was like a fish flung back. The first story I wrote, and I wrote it almost in one breath – about a cross-dresser buying new stilettos, then being fist-fucked by his boyfriend – was accepted immediately by a literary journal, and then I did it again, and again. I got a story into *Honcho*, then into *Inches*. The editors of those magazines gave me the confidence to keep writing. And although they were porn magazines, I have never written to titillate or excite. I write because I am baffled, in love, ecstatic.

By then I was in my mid-twenties, doing my degree at Tel Aviv University, taking a class in African-American Literature. That was my first encounter with Zora Neale Hurston, but I have a feeling it was before then, perhaps she was mentioned in the Intro to American Lit class the year before. And perhaps – I think Calvino said this – whenever we read a classic it is as if we have always known it. *Their Eyes Were Watching God* was an epiphany. Zora was the I-don't-give-a-fuck woman, I-go-where-I-want woman, dancing, tongue-in-cheek, to the band's narcotic harmonies. I was not going to be the white guy sitting there drumming the tabletop with my fingertips while everyone else worked themselves up into a frenzy. I would not be well-behaved. English Literature could not teach me this, Shakespeare could not teach me this, not Dickens, not Thackeray, not even Martin fucking Amis. I would be like Zora. I would tell my story the way I choose, juggle with this language my ancestors had barely heard of, pull it like toffee, make it sweet and brittle, knead it, roll in it, fuck it.

The first time I really thought about ways of doing it (writing), the first time I realised you could choose how to tell a story, that a writing voice was both refinable and innate (deep inside, there to discover), was when I read *Their Eyes Were Watching God*. Taking Hurston's lead, I became a kind of anthropologist, a participant-observer in my own world. I would write about my people, revel in variations of my self and its fictionalities, extract stories from the cryptic places I have access to, the cruising grounds, bathhouses, the bedrooms and clubs – in Tel Aviv, and eventually in Paris, London, Bangkok, Sydney, New York – those arenas of queer desire, the culture I was born into, initiated into by my peers and my own curiosity.

I was brought up by Xhosa women. I came into this world in Africa. There is that to think about when I think about Zora. And when I think about W.E.B. Du Bois and the double consciousness of black folk in a white West that "looks on in amused contempt and pity." Paule Marshall, Toni Morrison, Jean Toomer, Richard Wright, Langston Hughes: writers who spoke for a community but were and are completely individual, who gave me the tools to explore my otherness, gave me the language to write about what it meant to be me: a Jew in Africa, an immigrant in the Middle East, a queer person in this world, this "two-ness" that I carry, that if it wasn't for the dogged strength writing gives me, might tear me asunder.

Zora wrote until poverty and obscurity killed her, Kerouac until self-doubt and alcoholism defeated him, Preston was killed by AIDS. They were writers who, despite racism and homophobia and alcoholism and AIDS-phobia and self-loathing, said what they wanted to say in the way they wanted to say it. Their personal stories were the stories of a time in history, of their generation, their gang. The Harlem Renaissance, the Beats, Gay Liberation, the onset of the AIDS epidemic. They told their own stories first, and then they told the story of their folk, and through that, created a picture of a community and of themselves in it.

Our writing ancestors tell us about ways of dying, options available to us. I mean a trajectory, a path, as if the images we steppingstone our lives with foreshadow our ending, our death, and the ways in which we'll be remembered. But how can we know in the midst of all this violence, all this "contempt and pity," how and if we'll survive? We cling to the images of others to find our own direction, the image of a robust Canadian-American with a beret full of coins, a restless blackwoman with a notebook and fire, a cute young queerboy on a train going to meet his master.

Not just writers make us the writers we are. I owe the writer I am to others, too. To my father, who washed my mouth out with soap for standing on our front lawn and swearing randomly at passersby.

"Next time it'll be a jar of mustard," he said.

My father, a restless fisherman, frustrated poet and philosopher, lover of Jung and dream analysis, who gorged on books and psychology in the months of his dying. Twenty years before that, in the late 1970s when we left South Africa, he wrote letters home on weightless blue paper, his handwriting, like him, lean and upright, sharing the details of our new life. He left us with journals full of dread and rage, fuming and exorcising on the page the way his spiritual healer had told him to. "Write out the anger," he'd said to my dad, "then burn the pages." But my father kept them, or died before he could.

I have a high school teacher to thank for allowing me to write stories when I should have been writing essays for composition class. To the boyfriend who criticised my first attempts at stories, who said such disparaging things it took years to stop hearing his nasty voice. I thank him for being an obstacle that fortified me. And Isaac Rosenberg, mad mystical poet, who died long before I was born, a hundred years ago in the trenches near Arras, killed on April Fool's Day just months before the end of World War I. I was a boy when I heard them talking about him on the BBC World Service, listening on my barmitzvah-present radio in bed at night to the words of "Break of Day in the Trenches". A Jew who wrote poetry and got mentioned on the wireless. Who knew such a thing could exist?

And Agnes Makasi, maid and mother, who taught me that stories are told through the body, that we must lay ourselves bare if we want to be heard, if we want our stories to mean anything, speaking a language I could not understand, a language that relied on every part of the tongue, the whole of the mouth. Who showed me – we were in the kitchen one afternoon – a picture of a friend she'd grown up with in New Brighton. "She's in London," she said, awe and admiration in her voice for the friend who'd managed to escape to that epicentre of freedom, a sanctuary from the horrors of apartheid, and by extension – horror, in general. Bullies, homophobia, the homogeneity of the small town, war, political injustice. As if none of that could harm you, here, in London.

Marcos and Dan

Pete was cruel to Marcos. He beat him up a couple of times, tried to starve the dog, then one weekend he locked him in the flat without any food. You're getting a belly, he said to Marcos. It's disgusting. Pete freaked out whenever he thought Marcos was putting on weight.

Three months ago, Dan met Marcos, and although he'd never hurt him the way Pete did, he understands how it happens, how someone like Marcos can drive a guy crazy. Marcos likes it rough, likes to be slapped and spat on. He likes to be fucked hard.

"You make me tremble," he says, just at the point when Dan is getting scared Marcos will notice how desperate he is to disappear into him.

Dan hasn't been in love like this for a long time. If he had to say how long, he'd say ten years.

"I'm selfish," he says to Marcos. "I think only about myself."

"You're not selfish," Marcos says. "I know a lot of

selfish people and you're not one of them."

Marcos hasn't loved anyone for a long time, too. Pete doesn't count. Marcos says he's seen some of the evil things men do to each other, not in war but in love, the way men try to destroy each other. He knows about Dan's phobias, that every time he leaves the house he thinks he might die, snipers could get him, a bomb explode. Sometimes when he cycles over a Snickers wrapper he knows there could be a bomb inside. Dan says things when they're having sex, especially when he's inside Marcos, things like: I want to be like this forever and I love you, and reassures him it's just words, that it's not really what he wants, to trap him, that he just needs to say the words.

"I know, babe," Marcos says.

And so, last night, when they bump into each other at the sex club, they're both taken aback by how freaked out Dan is.

"But you always say you don't want anything."

"Of course I want things," Dan says. "I told you I wanted to see you tonight."

"You said you didn't want a boyfriend."

"I don't," Dan says. "But when I'm having sex with someone, there's responsibility."

They're standing at the top of the stairs while men pass to and from the shower area, and Dan feels like he might make a scene, that he might behave like the kind of person he hates: loud, irrational. Whining.

"I didn't mean to hurt you," Marcos says.

"Can we go somewhere?"

"It's late," Marcos says. "I need to go home. The dog."

"Did you have sex with a lot of guys?"

"Why do you ask that?"

"Just tell me."

They kiss, but Dan knows that if they fuck it'll be a mercy fuck. He can see Marcos wants to get away. But he doesn't care. He keeps the tone of his voice light, as if this is new, as if they've only just met. He keeps the conversation going

"When was the first time you had sex?" he says.

"You mean with a guy?" and tells Dan about the workers in his dad's factory back in Brazil, men who'd worked there for years, cut the fabrics, drove goods to the wholesalers, most were married to the seamstresses. He used to earn extra cash over the summers. When he left home at eighteen one of the guys helped him move, helped him paint the walls of his new place, carry up furniture. The man was at Marcos' disposal, so it was no surprise when they landed up having sex on the new bed.

"Those guys fuck anything," Marcos says.

"Did you do it more than once?"

"With that guy?"

"Were there others?"

"A lot," Marcos says. "But that guy came over once a week with food cooked by his wife."

"In exchange for this?" Dan says, and puts his finger inside Marcos, moves it back and forth, quickly, in jerking motions, so that it makes a wet sound.

"It's yours," Marcos says. "My pussy is yours."

Dan puts on a condom and fucks him and soon afterwards they come. They lie quietly for a few minutes, huddled together on the narrow bed in the cubicle, arms around each other.

"Now I really have to go, babe," he says.

When he leaves, Dan locks the cubicle door and lies there with a towel across his chest like a small blanket.

Dan is jealous – Marcos has things he wants: close friends, great teeth, healthy parents, a dog, a sister he's close to: they have the same tattoo on their lower backs, two dragons facing each other. Every year Marcos goes back to Brazil. When Dan first contacted him online Marcos was in Brazil, so they met when he got back to London.

"I almost didn't return," Marcos said.

Dan hardly talks about the war. Not because he's ashamed of being there, but he feels he wasn't a proper soldier. Dan got scared and was sent home, dismissed, released. They let him go. Dan's parents were in the police force. He grew up in a house with strict discipline. While he was training to be a nurse he joined the TA and then the army. The pay was good, he liked being outdoors. For years he'd been lucky – they didn't even send him to Northern Ireland, but then there was Afghanistan.

At the gym, Dan thinks of Marcos when some cute guy turns up in a green tracksuit top with BRAZIL on the back. He thinks about him when he's cycling to work through Islington, along Caledonian Road and passes the Brazilian café near the corner of Richmond Avenue. Dan knows Marcos doesn't think about him as much, that he's busy with work, with friends who come to stay. Marcos has a lot going on. He has friends in the countryside and in Torremolinos. He travels.

Marcos thinks about Dan when he's jerking off, his muscles, his chest, his fat cock. He thinks about him when Pete calls and says he wants to come over and see the dog. Marcos thinks: Text Dan to say you'll be late.

Dan leaves messages on Marcos' phone and on his Gaydar profile. He emails him. If he knew where he lived he'd go and check if he was there. Something might have happened. He could have gone to Brazil. Maybe he's had enough. Then one night Dan gets drunk and starts chatting to this guy on Gaydar who calls himself cumdump: suited on the outside, a pig on the inside. He's inviting guys – pos guys are better, he says – to come round to "fuck and fuck off." Dan pretends he is, and goes

Two weeks later Dan gets a text from Marcos. "I'm free this evening. Are you busy?"

Marcos asks if he can bring his dog. He says the dog doesn't like to be left alone.

When he turns up, they kiss the way they've always kissed and immediately they're naked in bed and Dan has a condom on and he's inside Marcos.

"Nobody fucks like you," Marcos says.

"I doubt that," Dan says.

"It's true. I am always happy when I see you."

"Are you?" Dan says.

"I love getting undressed for you," Marcos says.

"Why don't you ever tell me that?"

"I'm shy," he says.

"Of me?" Dan says, then he says, "You just disappeared?"

"I was fist raped for one whole weekend."

Pete had turned up with a little bag of coke.

"It wasn't like he forced me," Marcos said. "We used to do it once a year."

"Do you still do drugs?" Dan said.

"Never," Marcos said. "I promise. Not any more."

"But you did with Pete," Dan said.

"It's like a habit. Him and me and drugs."

Dan wants to know what happened. Marcos tells him that Pete put coke on his arsehole. It's that simple. He rubbed a bit into his arse so that Marcos couldn't feel how hard Pete was fisting him.

While Marcos talks, Dan strokes his chest, touches his nipples, presses his cock against Marcos' arse, so smooth and soft it's like it's been lubed up already. Dan spits quietly into his palm and wipes the spit against Marcos' crack. He fingers him gently. Marcos talks and Dan soothes him with his finger. He can tell Marcos is relaxed, he knows he feels safe with him.

At some point in the future, Frank will ask Dan what he was thinking.

"What was going through your head?" he'll say.

Dan will say he doesn't know, that he can't explain why he did it, but what was going through his head was this: It feels good to be fucking Marcos, to feel him loosen up so that there's no resistance, it's like being welcomed, and if only he could just keep going like this, these slow thrusts, everything will be fine.

"Come inside me," Marcos says.

"Are you sure," Dan says.

"I want you to," Marcos says.

"Say it again," Dan says.

Dan's inside him and Marcos says things like, I want you. You're my man. They both feel young, like boys, eager to fuck and get fucked, to be open and penetrable and reckless. And they both think: I am jumping off a cliff. I am sky-diving. They know they're taking a risk. They've survived so many deaths, never mind their own, and they've been through shit recently: Marcos' crazy weekend with his ex, Dan nearly losing it when he didn't hear from Marcos. And now there's this. One big guy with a big hairy chest and big hands and a big cock inside a cute slim guy and they are both so happy.

"Come inside me," Marcos says, "I trust you," and Dan keeps up the rhythm, Marcos all soft and warm, and he is about to come, full of love and anger and he knows that he shouldn't, he knows that what he's doing is bound to cause damage, but he just wants to hear the request, to hear Marcos say the words, invite him in, give himself to Dan. But Dan pulls out before he comes. He pulls his cock out and comes on Marcos' stomach, his smooth flat stomach, though by then it doesn't mater. The virus is in Marcos' blood, and in the next few weeks, just six months after they meet, Marcos and Dan will have to deal with the consequences of that night.

Foreigners in Sitges

Diego works in the breakfast room. He's into grunge, so I get extra points for being South African – apparently there's some famous grunge band from Durban. (What's grunge? But I don't ask.) I'm here in Sitges researching a book about painters who visited here in the 1920s. The hotel is on the seafront and you can hear the waves from the balcony.

"Foreigners in Sitges," Diego tells me in the evening at the hotel bar. "We stick together. Catalans don't like us."

He also tells me – *nah! really?* – that this is the gay capital of Spain. I listen to all this because he is beautiful. I am the kind of person who can endure a lot for the sake of beauty: boredom, repetition, torture, you name it. I'll devise endless questions to show my fascination, just to be close to men like Diego. Caught up in his beauty, I can't tell whether he's trying to seduce me, is just being nice, or is working for his tip. For the duration of my stay, Diego is the first man I see every morning, my first words of the day are to him.

One evening, he invites me to his gig at Marypili, a lesbian bar on Joan Tarrida. I sit close to the small stage and watch him swinging his locks, his headscarf around his neck, the music a mix of head-banging and Springsteen and it's sad and young and wild and yes, full of teen spirit. Every now and then he catches my eye and smiles in a way one smiles at admirers, the way he's probably seen men on screen smile at women who are in love with them. I feel vast and disloyal, as if you weren't waiting for me at home, as if I hadn't been having thoughts of you being The One.

We get drunk and land up at Diego's place where we have to be quiet because his flatmates are asleep and what lands up happening is that when he dozes off with a joint in his hand, I lift his T-shirt and trace the treasure trail down to his pubes, and when his cock gets hard, I put it in my mouth and suck until he comes and I swallow and he sighs and in just a few seconds he's breathing slowly, snoring lightly. And I sit there smiling to myself, because it's been years (twenty-two, to be exact) since I've fooled around with a straight boy. I watch him sleep, his body unguarded, his stomach exposed, thick pubic hair, cock soft and plump and shining with spit.

I take the circuitous route back to the hotel to increase my chances of picking someone up, which I do, a waiter who lives with his boyfriend and is out for a late-night stroll with their dog. We jerk each other off in an alleyway in the old part of town, our cum dotting the cobblestones.

Straight boys like to show you things, and of those, the ones without fathers the most. Look what I've made, Daddy. Look what I've found. The young man teaches the older man about grunge, eager to introduce him to the soundtrack of his life. There is something very close to sublime about the body of a young man almost twenty years younger than you. It's a new thing I'm discovering, now that I'm at an age where the world is overflowing with grown men much younger than me.

Diego has come up to my room so he can play me The Banx on his iPod dock. We're stoned and naked and it's three in the morning. He lies on the bed staring up at the ceiling and I kneel beside him, my head level with his body. He is silent and I am silent, there is nothing to say. I can tell from his eyes, from the way his mouth is shut, that he is beyond caring. The streetlamps cast a dull light onto everything – his skin, the bed linen, the wallpaper – a kind of doughy yellow.

"It's not going to work," he says.

"What's wrong with the way it is?"

"It's not what I want," he says, and turns onto his side to look at me, his locks fanning out across the pillow like a kid's drawing of the sun's rays.

"Why did you come up?" I say.

"I like being with you," he says.

"Then why can't we keep doing this?" I say.

I gather his hair into a sheaf so that his face and neck are exposed.

"You want more than I can give," he says.

"You have to fuck someone," I say. "So why not let it be me?"

"I don't," he says, and turns back to face the ceiling. "Now stop, please."

"Okay," I say. "Can I lie next to you?"

He moves over to make room for me on the bed. I tell him about one of the painters I'm writing about, a man who killed himself in his late forties, around the time of his son's seventh birthday. I tell him he used to come to Sitges with his wife and other writers and painters, that he'd tried to meet Picasso, but Picasso had taken the train back to Barcelona before he had the chance to see him. Eventually we fall asleep, Diego facing one way, me the other, the edges of our bodies touching.

In the morning – just three hours sleep! – the sun comes up over the sea and shines onto the bed. The only sound is waves, their metronomic lapping, gently falling and falling. Diego goes downstairs for breakfast duty and I sit on the edge of the bed and watch the water and the palm-trees beyond the balcony's railings. A man cycles along the promenade to work. People walk their dogs on the shore. The sea is calm and silver, the sun so bright the water dazzles. In the distance there's a dark smudge: a boat? a clump of seaweed? seagulls? light playing tricks on water? The landscape is celadon and aquamarine. In the pots on the edge of the balcony, the gerberas are bright yellow. Soon I'll be home again. You'll be there to meet me. Diego will do breakfast and play grunge for the lesbians. From the room next door I can hear what sounds like a couple making early-morning love.

The Homo Daddy's Guide to Lovemaking

Call him things like: My baby. My sweet baby. Tell him that his sweet body is yours now. He has never been anyone's boy before, but it's as if he's been waiting for this for a long time. Be his daddy. Listen when he tells you: "I'm usually the one who does the fucking." Say to him: "Do you like it like this now?" You are inside him and he looks calmer and more content than ever. You've known him for three weeks, though it feels like longer. He's a DJ, tall and Latin brown. You like tall skinny men. You like tall skinny men with long hair. You met him at a friend's exhibition, a painter who's been doing a series of pieces about the club scene in London. Your boy had posed for her with his long brown hair that falls down his back, and his thick metal earrings and his shirt off, and the swallow in flight on his chest. If a dozen things were different he'd look like James Dean, but he has that same wild, wiry energy. Tell him how peaceful he looks.

Wonder if this calmness you bring is not too confusing, a result of your need to control him. You have been known to want to control. You are not unlike many of us who have grown up unloved. Your shiatsu guy says you should go dancing twice a week. "Even in your living room," he says. "Get more movement into your body." He says you've got muscle mass but it's become stagnant. "Stagnation," he says, "is a word often used in shiatsu." And you think, as you go in and out of your boy, making him happy, that this must be the perfect movement, the perfect flowing gesture, this gentle back and forth in and out of another human being – the most soothing and crazy-making... just fucking crazy-making... part of your body inside the body of another human. Hold him from behind. Hold him close to you. Your boy against his daddy. Press your stomach to his back. Don't move. Feel the bulk of your stomach against the concave of his back, then start that gentle back and forth again. "Is that nice? And he says: "Make love to me, papi. I want you to make love to me." For a moment, think that these words might scare you into softening, that too much tenderness might put you off, but the hunger in his voice keeps you hard and makes you enfold him, raise him onto all fours so his hands are on the wall and you are holding him, spooning, big C to little c, the opening of quotation marks: "You're my baby. My beautiful baby," And he says, yes, he says, yes, he says: "Make love to me." You cannot see his face, but you know his eyes are closed and he is easing himself into this newfound role, this place he has not been before. "Why did you come to me at the exhibition? What made you talk to me?" Smile when he says: "*You* talked to *me*." You like it when he calls you "Professor." You like the way his body fits into yours, like a Russian doll. He is skin and bone. You are his shell and flesh. Enjoy the way your boy pushes himself back onto you so that you can go deeper. Wrap your arms around his chest and pull him to you. Roll onto your back and carry him with you so that he lies on your chest, his long hair falling into your face, his back against your front, your back on the bed. Thrust into him. You like that word: Thrust. You like words like shove and ram and bang. Say these words. Think about banging and thrusting and slamming into him. And do it. Lift his whole body with your body and push into him with each upward movement, and as you come back onto the bed pull him against you. Keep your arms around him. Tell him: "Arch your back," so he can press against you, draw you deeper into him. You have been told you are good at this. Some men call you especially for this, just because you do this to them: make them feel like your boy. You were never a daddy before your father died. Back then, you were the age your boy is now. It's just a game this thing between you and your boy. You can tell when you are pleasing a man, when your boy is happy. Say: "Sit on me." Say: "Let me see your face." Press your palms against the tight skin of his back as he lifts himself off your chest. Hold him tightly to stay inside while he slowly turns to face you. Watch his expression change as he says: "Don't take it out. No, no, no, don't take it out." That expression on the edge of abandonment. Say: "My god, you are beautiful." Think how in just under an hour – or has it been longer? – you've gone through six different positions. Ha, movement! you think, as you think of your shiatsu guy. Nothing stagnant about this. Feel proud of yourself. Feel amazed at how a fag like you who has gone through a childhood like yours... think how you are now a big fucking homo daddy. A pleasurer of boys. Enjoy the sensation of being inside someone and satisfying him. Feel wonder at how your body has developed in a way that has... in a way that... and all the time you're thinking these thoughts, urge your boy to keep moving like that. Say: "Use me to pleasure yourself. It's all for you, baby." Until he comes on your chest. Beautiful warm ribbons that reach your neck and your face and the pillow to the side of your head. Watch him breath and smile and his chest rise and fall and the dark-green tattoo of the swallow rise with it. Let him straighten his legs and lie on you, his body against yours, cupped in yours, the largeness of you. Say to him: "You're still hard." And he'll say, yes, that's what you do to me, and he'll put his mouth close to your ear and whisper: "Now open up." He'll whisper in your ear:

"It's your turn." And you do, because you like opening up to men who want to be inside you, who want to know you, who'll rename you with terms of endearment like: Baby. Like: Professor. Like: Daddy.

Three French Men

The Cubicles

Number One would not kiss. His height and his body and his skin and his face and everything was just right – but in the steam room, he turned his head when I leaned in. An inch taller than me, his cock hard and upright, hair black, pale skin. Number One was so skinny that when I put my arms around him I could reach my own shoulders, as if there was nothing there. He whispered (in French): *Let's go into a cubicle where we can be alone*. I assume that's what he said when we left the steam room and he turned to see if I was following. Number One held my hand as he led me upstairs and into a cubicle, though we did not last very long. He seemed disappointed when I motioned to leave the cubicle. I didn't explain why I was leaving. (I rarely do.) I didn't say much except "*Ouevre la porte*." If I'd been at home, in London, which is now my home, but far from everywhere I come from, I'd have said: "I rely on your lips against mine." Something to make it clear that kissing was part of fucking. For Number One, kissing was not part of it. Number One would not kiss. He was tall and skinny (my favourite) and would have been the one I'd have wanted the most. But I cannot bear the desertion of a kiss refused. Nor did he smile.

The Steam Room

Number Two liked to kiss very much. Number Two kissed with hungry enthusiasm. He stood on tip-toes to kiss me. Number Two was short enough to suck my nipples from a standing position. He had the fattest cock. He was also the darkest – he could have been Portuguese, so many Portuguese men I've met have very large cocks. Number Two liked sex a lot, he was into it, as opposed to needing someone to help him get off. He tried to lick my arse, but I hadn't showered and I'd been shitting all morning (foreign cities make me nervous) but the real reason is that it takes me a while before I offer my arse to strangers. Number Two spoke to me in English, perhaps it was the couple of times I said, yeah, yeah, or maybe he couldn't speak French either. Maybe he was Portuguese.

Number Two was a koala bear. He kissed with gusto, the way he did everything, the way he made me pick him up so he could wrap his legs around me and rest his elbows on my shoulders. He didn't care that there was no visible sign of my arousal. But he was nice to kiss and he had the kind of cock men take pictures of alongside an aerosol can or a can of Coke. His was like a can of Coke.

We were in the steam room, having both warded off the advances of a man who'd been going around touching everyone like in some lethargic game of tag. I, too, was desperate for physical contact, and the wonder of Number Two's cock was a comfort and a pleasure. It had the reassurance of an anchor. Number Two kept saying fuck me, fuck me, until the heat in the steam room became so unbearable we doused ourselves in cold water under the shower by the door.

When Number Two came (I'm assuming that's what the sound was) we kissed, and he said take care (in English). Number Two might have smiled, but it was dark and misty and I wasn't wearing my glasses, though going by his wholehearted behaviour, I wouldn't be surprised if Number Two, when we parted, was smiling.

The Dry Sauna

I was about to head back to my hotel, so Number Three was unexpected. He was so perfect in his body, his thuggish good looks, that I didn't insist on kissing. Kissing could wait. I was happy to adore, to be the supplicant. Number Three wanted someone to help him get off: his was the kind of beauty people wanted to service. Number Three said very few words: *non* and Stefan were two of them.

He showed very little interest. A friend of mine says indifference is a very French trait; that they reserve their enthusiasm for food and ideas. But I need enthusiasm when I'm having sex. I need that wide-eyed, effusive energy from my lovers, proof that my being there and their being there at that moment in time is a great joy. Enthusiasm is a form of cosmic gratitude.

But I make exceptions.

Sometimes my enthusiasm is enough for two.

In the case of Number Three, my enthusiasm was enough for both of us.

I'd been sitting on the wooden slats in the sauna and I'd been thinking: Number One and Number Two were fine. But third time lucky. Number Three was my third-time-lucky. He'd entered the dry sauna because of me. He'd seen me through the window in the sauna door. But I can't be sure of that, maybe he was planning to come in anyway. He had tiny scars on his face, pockmarks, though it's hard to be precise about that kind of thing without my glasses. He positioned himself at the opposite end of the sauna, a couple of metres away from me, and leaned against the wall, his body taut and muscled, his white towel around his waist.

Earlier that morning, I'd seen men like him hanging on the walls of the Palais des Beaux Arts: Ribot's St Vincent amongst the crows and the wolf, the saint's naked body the only source of light in the painting, thin brushstrokes of black in the centre of his beige chest, his red nipples, Achilles in Bastien-Lepage's *Priam aux pieds d'Achille*, the two men's fingers touching, Priam distressed, old and ragged, and Achilles upright in a loin-cloth, gold chain around his ankle.

Number Three glared at the wall opposite him and at me on the wooden slats staring back at the outline of his cock beneath his towel. At that moment, I was every single gay boy who's ever stared at the locker-room demigods, undeserving, yet unwavering in their devotion. And I thought: Even if nothing happens, I have been this close, alone in a room with a man whose beauty is pornographic. Sometimes it's enough to be a witness. I do not masturbate to pornography, but I did masturbate in the presence of Number Three.

Then someone walked in.

Not all interruptions are bad.

This interruption was bad.

A tall guy, so young, still with puppy fat, sits down and runs his hands through his hair, rests his elbows on his knees and sighs a very deep sigh to let us know he is old enough to be jaded: all this is too much effort, but I endure for the greater good. He is awkward and harmless and he's detracting from the scenario we've been working on. So I left. And I turned at the door to look at Number Three, who was not yet Number Three, just A Beautiful Thug, and our eyes met.

I would get what I wanted.

I love these places.

If Number Three had been Number Two, the dark enthusiast from twenty minutes ago, he'd have followed *tout de suite*. With Number Two there'd have been no need to test anything. He and I had stayed in the steam room, never went anywhere (I rarely do). At some point we'd stood under cold water and his cock had stayed hard: further proof of his keenness. The water had been an oasis of cool in the thick heat of the steam room, where I now sit and wait for Number Three.

Waiting is not always an aphrodisiac. It belittles. It can be the demeaning evidence of your powerlessness. Waiting for Number Three was none of these. It gave me time to imagine the curves of his chest, their firmness, the smoothness of his skin, the weight of his cock in my mouth, its saltiness. Waiting is part of hunting, it heightens the pleasure, fuels the imagination. Other types of waiting damage the soul, lead to despair and loss of hope: waiting for money, for recognition, to be discovered, rescued, called upon – these are types of waiting I have known.

But I do not give up easily.

"No" is not something I like to take for an answer.

I went back to the dry sauna.

In my absence, Number Three had moved from one end to the other, and was leaning against the wall beside the bench I'd been sitting on. I took up the same position, picked up from where I'd left off, resumed playing with my cock. I stared at his body, his flat stomach, his hidden belly-button, his smooth tanned skin, his erect nipples, confronted the menacing look. I built up the courage to lean over, like this, cautiously, to touch him. He's going to hit me. He hates himself and hates his sexuality (he's a builder, a plumber, a garbage-collector), full of contempt for the *pédés* of this world. He's here to show his disgust. I would make fear my aphrodisiac. All those things that stifle and undermine me (fear, indifference, waiting) would keep me hard.

I touched him the way you touch something rarely seen in nature. I touched him the way you touch a sacred object, tentatively, because I thought: If this is all I get, at least I will carry it in my fingertips, this memory of the velvet flesh, the steel of his muscle. I will remember the awe his body inspired in me. I will forget nothing.

When I tried to unclasp his towel, Number Three left the sauna room and made sure I was following: we turned right, then round the corner, up the stairs, into the first cubicle on the left. Only then, facing each other, did I notice how short he was. Number Three was the shortest of all. Also the most beautiful. I treated him like a porn star. From the way he spread his towel on the thin vinyl mattress, then lay back and offered his arse, it was clear what Number Three was after. But I'm not good at fucking in saunas, and definitely not after two hours of sweating and cold showers and fiddling around with Number One and Two. I'm sure there are men whose ability and desire to fuck would be heightened by these factors and by the fact that Number Three was quick to recline, raise his legs, and expose himself. I am not like most men. I have very specific issues. Many of them have to do with waiting.

Number Three was not interested in conversation. He had an arsehole that needed licking.

Number Three came while I licked his balls and fingered him, his cum arcing onto his stomach. I wanted to lick it up, to catch it on my tongue, it seemed the right thing to do. I thought of you back at home, and I thought how easy it is to take risks, how easy not to. I stayed on my knees jerking myself off, pressing my nipple against his thigh, and while he played with his cock, I came on the floor.

I kissed his stomach, spread his cum across his torso, rubbed it in with his sweat. He had bristles in the concave between his nipples. The rest of his body was smooth: his legs, his thighs, everything. His cock was still hard in his fist.

"*Encore*?" I said.

"*Non*," he said.

He might have smiled at this point, but I cannot be sure.

"What's your name?" I said.

"*Quoi?*"

"*Comment tu t'appelle?*" I said.

I thought he might ask for mine.

But that was all Stefan said. Three words. I said *merci*. He smirked when I said that. I did not have my glasses on, so I could be mistaken, it might have been a smile.

If this had been London, if this had been the city I've made my home, I'd have initiated a conversation, kept flirting with Number Three, complimented him on his body, on the way he massaged my shoulders for just a few second while I sucked his cock. But my poor vocabulary makes me reticent, makes me hold back, turns me silent. When he left, I stayed in the cubicle and lay on the thin mattress. I thought about the dream I'd woken from that morning: In it I'd watched a man get beaten up by another man. The attacker had ordered his Rottweiler to bite into the victim's hands and keep them behind his back so the attacker could punch the man's face. The victim's boyfriend looked on. I shouted police, police, and even though there was a squad car parked outside the Chinese restaurant, no one came to help.

I remember waking up thinking that I was the victim, the boyfriend, the thug, the Rottweiler and the indifferent policemen. It's not often that I remember my dreams, which made me think that perhaps the dream was a foreshadowing. For a while I thought Number Three was going to punch me, that I was going to be the cowardly boyfriend and the Rottweiler who made it all possible. I wouldn't have fought back (I rarely do).

Later, sitting in the bar area drinking Schweppes Limon, I watched two soldiers capture a young man at gunpoint and make him strip. One of the soldiers used his cock to slap the prisoner's face, and then made him suck it. The guns were M16 rifles. The bartender asked me if I'd been out that day, that it looked as though I'd caught some sun. I told him I'd been at the art gallery that morning, then had lunch in a café on Place Béthune. The lemonade was cool and sweet as it made its way down my gullet. The second soldier took his cock out of his trousers and inserted it into the prisoner's arse. Behind them was a bombed-out building with clusters of grass sprouting from the cracks in its wall. Then I spotted Number One, heading for the jacuzzi, and we locked eyes. I nodded, and from where I was sitting, even though I was not wearing my glasses, I was sure he nodded back.

La Lokal, Lille, Friday, 25 August, 2006.

Jack Kerouac Is the Buddha

He says I remind him of Neal, my wiry body, the way my eyes dart all over the place. You don't talk as much as he does, he says. That guy keeps going. But he's beautiful, man, Jack says. Beautiful from the inside out. He talks as if we've spoken before, made our introductions years back, and now we're friends catching up after way too long apart. The music is loud and I'm finding it hard to hear what Jack's saying. He's got his top off and it's distracting. My eyes move from his dark hair to his arms, his torso, the buckle of his belt. He smiles like he knows what I'm thinking, but he's not about to make the first move.

"Are you sure we've never spoken before?" he says.

"I'm sure," I say.

"But I've seen you around," he says.

"Yes," I say. "You probably have."

When we get home, I show him my copy of *On the Road*,

bought back in the late 1970s, the 1957 Signet edition, the cover a bright yellow sun on an orange background. Jack's name in a fat sans-serif font. The pages are crumbling, flimsy, bits detaching like plaster from a wall. He's not interested, opening and closing cupboards, looking in the fridge, flicking back his mop of hair, splashing cold water on his face. He tries to undo my trousers, unbutton my shirt. Wait, I say. Look at this. Even when I bought the book it looked used, yellowed. It was the last copy on the shelf in that branch of Steimatsky's on Dizengoff Street, as if it had been sitting there since the 1950s. On the inside cover, I've written 1981 – I was eighteen. A year later I went into the army, more or less the same age Jack was when they kicked him out for being psychotic.

"You never wrote anything as good as this," I say.

"Not a lot of love in that statement." he says, the corner of his mouth turned up, eyes rolled back. "For someone who can hardly get his first book done, you're doing a lot of criticising."

"We're similar," I say. "Still stuck on our first love."

"Is there anything to eat in this fucking house?"

"This book," I say, pressing it against his chest, our lips almost touching, "is a love poem to Neal Cassidy. The man you couldn't tame."

"That's harsh," Jack says, turning away, his back an invitation to follow, his voice a jazz whisper.

"Harsh," I say. "But true."

For a long time I thought it was Jack's book that I loved, but really it was the Ann Charters biography of him, the one she wrote in exile in Sweden. I read it in my room at the top of the house, that summer in the furnace room, before air-conditioning, bonfires blazing on the threshold. I slept on piled-up mattresses, safe from the evil spirits. The biography was a thick book with a painting of Jack on the cover, solemn, bright blue shirt, green vest, black hair coiffed for the picture, Brylcreamed. In her introduction, Ann Charters writes about leaving the US during the war in Vietnam, and I like to think of my move to London as being in that tradition. Exile as protest. Baldwin in Paris, Hemingway, Joyce.

When I came to London in the 1990s, the first guy I dated was obsessed with the Beat Generation, stuck in the 50s, that decade before we were born. I didn't like his whole poverty script, so while he stayed at home and smoked pot, played his guitar, composed lyrics about love, but mainly sang songs from the boring Beatles, I worked as a janitor in a school, tended bar in a nightclub in Covent Garden. I lived with Tom for six months. I don't think he really noticed when I left. But I miss those weekends in bed, high on skunk, him copying Picasso sketches, me reading aloud from *Doctor Sax* and *Visions of Cody*. We'd get up at midday and go to the Star Express for breakfast: egg and chips, bacon, sausages, black pudding, mushrooms, hash browns, grilled tomatoes.

"And then?" Jack says.

"We'd crawl back into bed."

"That's a big breakfast." Jack says.

"Are you hungry?" I say.

"Not anymore," he says. "But I'm ready to crawl back into bed."

"More tequila first," I say. "I'll line up the shots."

While Jack snores, I lie awake thinking about helping him get stronger, getting him off the booze and Benzedrine. I'm a good boy from a good home and I have a lot of love to offer. It's a sexual thing between Jack and me. He lets me fuck him when he's drunk, full of shame about Mémère. Sometimes he likes to joke about what we're doing, other times he refuses to talk about it. I go along with whatever. He's helping me with stuff, too, bringing more abandon and danger into my life. When I was a kid, he taught me about freedom and setting off on journeys with no clear destination. He kept me sane during the war. We have a similar relationship to our mothers. The only difference is that Jack and Mémère still get drunk together and land up falling asleep in the same bed.

We met in a club off Tottenham Court Road.

"I've never been here before," he said, like he was trying to justify something, as if he was worried I'd run out and tell the papers, spoil the attention he's been getting in Paris where everyone is head of heals in *amour avec lui*. "This place is foul," he said.

"Yeah," I said. "I love it. It's the only place where you can't smell the encroaching stink of Christmas. Do you mind if I smell your armpits?"

I wanted to prove a point, that I wasn't all talk. Jack giggled. If the club hadn't been so dark and dingy, I'm sure I'd have seen him blush.

"You guys," he said. "You're like fucking pigs," and laughed louder this time, head thrown back, mouth wide, arms in the air like I'd threatened to shoot him. "I give up. I totally fucking give up."

I touched his crotch and he didn't say no. I whispered: Jack. And he whispered: What? I said: Jack. He said: What's your name,? So I told him.

"That's a nice Irish name," he said. "I like the Irish."

I played along.

Jack was impressed when I took him all the way to the base. Edie could never have done that. In fact, he said, flopping down on some manky sofa, exhausted, unable to come, no woman has ever done that. What? I said. That, he said. Say it. Fuck off, he said. So I got up and went to the bar to fetch more tequilas, enough to make us happy, enough to convince Jack to come home with me.

In the dream it's 2001 at City Lights Bookstore and we're

waiting for Ginsberg and Ferlinghetti to read. Jack is zigzagging through the crowd, beret in hand, collecting small change to buy bottles of red wine. He's calmer on the drugs and the booze. He's sleeping better. Nothing is too much when he's like this – until, that is, it all gets too much and he wants to keep going, keep writing – write it all out of himself. He tells me he's lost interest in what he has to say, that there's nothing left to say, that whenever he opens his mouth everything comes out false. So he's going to stop opening his mouth, he doesn't want to hear himself speak, what he has to say is of no consequence.

"I've lost touch with too many people," he says.

But then, just before daybreak, there he is, naked at the typewriter, whiskey in his tumbler, pounding out Proustian sentences on rolls of shelf-paper. I stand behind him and massage his shoulders, press into the top of his back, his thick neck, and try to ease the tension.

"I'm not tense," he says. "I'm on a roll."

"Then keep rolling," I say.

"That's my coccyx," he says. "Don't press so hard."

"I'm going to write all this down," I say. "Exactly how it happened."

"I'd rather you didn't," he says. "It doesn't show me in a positive light."

"You're the one who went traipsing after Ginsberg to the baths."

"Can you stop for a second?" Jack says.

So I come up for air, kissing his stomach, pressing my nose into the sparse hair in the valley between his nipples. Jack turns to face the curtains, as if he can see beyond them to the dawn sky, the seascape of white clouds.

"I used to let Neal do that," he says.

"And Caroline?"

"Caroline, too," he says. "It was the only way to hold onto him, and keep him away from Alan. I thought if I let him, if I made love to Caroline… shared his girl with him… my best guy and my best gal, then..."

"Jack," I say.

"Wait," he says. "Let me finish."

It's getting bright outside, but neither of us moves to open the curtains. We listen to Mémêre in the kitchen moving pots around, opening and closing drawers. It's her way of letting us know she's hungry and wants company, that it's time to stop doing what we're doing and help her put food on the table.

"One more thing," he says, pausing at the door. "I've been thinking. Maybe I hung out with all those fags – Neal and Bill and Alan – so they'd fall in love with me, so I could work out whether that's what I wanted."

"Just so you could say no."

"I'm sick of saying no," he says.

"Tell me more about your misadventures," I say.

"More like pissadventures," he says.

"But us," I say. "What we have is good."

"What we have is disgusting."

I put on my sad face.

"But it makes me feel like Proust," he says. "Like Melville, the incarnation of Rimbaud."

"You're the Buddha, Jack."

"I am," he says. "I'm a fucking dharma bum."

He comes back to sit on the edge of the bed, daylight filtering through the curtains. It feels like weeks since we last saw direct sunlight, like we've been stuck in some kind of diurnal purgatory, trapped behind glass. He's winding down, but I can barely keep my eyes open, to fall asleep would be to abandon him.

"Jack, I need to get out," I say.

"Go," he said. "Just fucking go."

I curl up behind him and slide my hand up the back of his T-shirt, press my fingers along the ridges of his spine.

"I'm tense," he says.

"Lie back," I say. "I'll calm you. If you don't get some sleep, you'll turn to stone."

At breakfast, Mémêre is sulking. Jack's twitching and it's hard to tell if he's nodding off or just wants to get back to his typewriter. Mémêre looks at me and says I remind her of someone, though she can't remember *qui*.

"Neal?" I say.

"No," she says, "Definitely not him."

"I think I should go," I say.

"*Oui*," Mémêre says. "*C'est un très bon idée.*"

"Call me," Jack says.

I take the slice of toast from his plate, shrug, dare him, but he's oblivious, focused on his cheese omelette, slicing it with the side of his fork. Mémêre must be watching but I don't look her way. I walk to the door and out into the morning light and head towards the main road, past the terraced houses, the small council estate, the newsagent. The air is so crisp it's like thin ice, the traffic a constant stream of cars and lorries. They whoosh by, all of them heading somewhere, away from here. All of them could take me with them, so I hold out my hand, my thumb in the air, and wait for someone to stop.

The Man in the Pool

I don't like the way he looks at my son, the way he stares, no matter where we are or what Julian's doing, but particularly here where it's warm and in the evenings we swim in the hotel's indoor pool. The man has no idea how young my son is, if he knew, he'd be ashamed to be ogling a fifteen-year-old boy, but Julian's oblivious, doing his laps, drying himself, texting his friends, mildly embarrassed to be on holiday in Spain with his father and me. We're here for a week to get away from the fire that burnt down our business. When we get back, we'll start over. Julian knows nothing about the fire. We agreed to tell him when we're home again. He's doing well at school, top marks in Spanish, so this trip to Almería is his reward.

The pool's big enough for ten strokes a length and the man and my son cover the pool from one end to the other in a couple of breaths, as if they've silently agreed on a race. The man must be my age, maybe older, his back broad, his hair dark and straight. My son could be his son, but the man does not look at him the way a father looks at a son. The sound of their hands and feet against the water echoes in the enclosure. My husband is upstairs reading before dinner, detective novels and crime thrillers, books easy on the mind.

"I want to forget," Mark says.

The fire had come out of nowhere. It could have been a fuse or something left on overnight. The reason isn't important, there'd been a fire and the place had burnt down. The fire engines arrived after we did – too late to save anything. The whole thing is a blessing in disguise, although I do not say this to Mark. This is our first holiday in ten years, and when we get home we're making changes, using the insurance money to do what we really want to do, leaving the city, moving somewhere quiet.

I can tell by the way the man moves his head, as if to breathe, that he's staring at Julian's body, ogling him underwater, head to the side, as he passes my son.

Julian stops at the shallow end and stands up.

"Claudette," he says.

"Yes, son," I say.

"Is it time to eat yet?"

The man keeps swimming, somersaulting with each turn, pushing himself off the side with such force I'm afraid he'll collide with Julian as he stands there in the pool calling out to me.

After dinner, my husband and I make love. His body is firm and strong and solid and he smells of coconut oil. When we kiss I taste the evening's salmon on his breath, his mouth is big and his tongue heavy, everything about him is warm and determined. I wonder if this is the kind of body Julian will have when he grows up, for now he is slim and agile, taller than boys his age, taller than my husband. His height makes people think he's older than he is. They serve him in pubs.

The smell of the sea is comforting, the sound of the waves, white strips of them flopping onto the shore. Julian sleeps at the far end of the corridor and for the moments that this worries me, he might as well be on the other side of the world, teaching English in the Andes, backpacking in Tanzania, wrenched from me.

"You're restless," Mark says.

"It's too humid to sleep,"

"Turn on the air conditioning."

"I'll be fine."

He kisses my cheek and turns onto his side, this man who can sleep through anything. It's November, and although the nights are cool, the days are still warm and good for the beach, the sun bright and hot so that by the end of the day we're tired and the breeze is pleasant on the skin. As my husband's breathing slows, I listen to the quiet intake and exhalation of air, feel myself drifting off, soothed by the rise and fall next to me and the sound of waves, and I wish for my son this kind of companionship and the calming sea and I imagine stroking his head and whispering, sleep, my baby boy, like I've whispered to him many times before.

In the morning, my husband and I eat alone, a breakfast of fresh fruit, toast with jam and cheese, coffee. I don't mention anything about the man who looks at our son, even though he's sitting opposite us, close to the big windows, sun shining in over the sea and onto his table. I like the ease of this place, the light so bright that even in autumn it seems to bleach the buildings, parch everything, peeling plaster, dust from the desert. Wild bougainvillea growing everywhere.

In today's paper there's an article about a girl who jumped from the window of her hotel in Prague. The article says her father raped her several times a year from when she was five until she turned thirteen. Two days ago was her nineteenth birthday, the day before that she was about to win a chess tournament. People said it was the stress of the finals, but then they found a recording she'd made one night with friends, all of them drunk, and her recounting what her father had done.

How does a father not kill himself after that, follow in his daughter's footsteps and leap from a window to the pavement? The girl died in a foreign city where she wouldn't be recognised by passers-by, as if she could walk off the face of the earth.

"You know we love you," I say to Julian.

"Yes, Claudette," he says. "I know that."

Last night in the lobby, the older guests were playing bingo, a crowd in their seventies on a package holiday, Spanish tourists from somewhere in Spain. They made me happy, this band of pensioners, cocooning me in a language I couldn't understand, lulled by the clean smell of chlorine from the decorative pools in the lobby, lively Spanish music, and the sound of birds from the aviaries. The young bingo caller with her straight black hair and tight orange top shifting her gaze when Julian walks towards me, smiling at him. He'd been in the Business Centre checking emails.

We ordered *dos cervezas* and a *jamón* and cheese sandwich from the waiter.

"The bus leaves at ten tomorrow," I say. "It'll be a fun trip."

"I'm fine just staying here," he says.

"Are you happy, Julian?" I say.

"What do you mean?"

"Here," I say. "In general."

"Oh, definitely," he say. "Ecstatic."

We both laugh, an hysterical kind of laughter, for the absurdity of the question. The laughing melts something, softens us, and I feel the warmth of having known each other for so long.

I have known this boy all his life.

Which is when I tell him about the fire.

"We'll be making changes."

"What kind of changes?"

"We'll talk about it," I say. "The three of us."

The waiter approaches and we order two more bottles, and when they come they are cold and sweet and we drink in silence. It's like a lesson in learning the numbers in Spanish.

"She's got a nice voice," I say. "Very pretty."

"*Basta*," he says.

When the game is over, the barman turns the music down and the old people file back to their rooms, the stage stands empty like something abandoned. The young woman has disappeared, smuggled out by her audience.

"Call the boy," my husband says. "He'll miss breakfast."

"Have you seen this story?"

I hand him the paper. I open a serviette and wrap two croissants and little tubs of jam, golden nuggets of butter.

"The bus leaves in an hour," I say.

The waiters smile and say *buenos días* as I leave the dining room and take the lift up to the third floor where my son is waking up.

The bus from Almería to the old town of Mojácar crosses through the desert, past roundabouts similar to the ones in Baghdad that we've seen on the news as American soldiers entered the city. In the middle of the roundabouts: tall white arches and statues, large stick men, bright white against the pale sky, like a child's drawing of a man, a long line for the body, two shorter ones for the arms and legs, a circle for the head, and above the head, a semi-circle like an archer's bow.

The desert is vast and open, and the dry air through the window is warm on my face.

I was fourteen when it happened. He was older, from another school. After we'd done it I asked for a cigarette. It felt like the right thing to do. An actress on a bed in a movie. We smoked without saying anything and he didn't ask if I was okay or how it was. He was slight, not much bigger than me, and I vowed to always be with men who could shield me.

The paper said it always happened just after her birthday, unlucky to be born when the nights are long, when darkness keeps people at home and allows things like that to happen. How does anyone write the story of a child entered by her father? Are men allowed to write these stories after the things they do?

She was not a virgin on her first day of school.

How does one continue after that?

If the father is to blame, then others are to blame, too. Let them all stand on the ledge of the hotel in Prague and prepare, like divers, to hit the ground. Take them all with you, precious girl. Take them all. The father who did it while the mother slept – or in the mornings when she was at work, always in the girl's bed, the father's hand over her mouth, his breath...

The cinnamon stink of Christmas.

Death was the girl's only escape. She jumped to save herself.

Before the bus turns towards the beach, we get off and head into Mojácar la Vieja, the old town. The first attraction is the public fountain at the foot of the hill. Water spouts from the wall, and the locals fill their plastic containers from the mountain spring, thick cold water, and it's when I bend down to drink that my back clenches, a sharp pain from my tailbone all the way down my leg.

"Claudette," my husband says. "Sit for a bit."

"Better to keep moving," I say.

We climb towards the top of the old town, the steep winding streets, stopping at the observation point to look out over the desert, the dusty shrubs, construction work everywhere, and in the distance rows of white houses close to the beach, beyond that – the sea. Julian walks ahead of us, his steps animated, light, and suddenly I want to collapse onto a bench and weep. To have brought this into the world, so pure, destined to leave. I have given life to this boy so, in return, he can give me lessons in grief and loss.

"I told him about the fire," I say to Mark.

"How did he take it?"

"I said there'll be changes."

"What kind of changes?"

"I don't know," I say.

"Are you okay, Claude?" he says.

"It's good we've come away for a bit," I say.

In a gift shop at the top of the hill we buy fridge magnets with little versions of the stick men, the shape of the statues we'd seen on the roundabouts. For good luck, the woman in the shop tells us, and we notice on the way down that the houses have similar tiles on their walls to ward off evil spirits. Mark and I hold hands, and I want to give my other hand to Julian, to be flanked by my men, but I know it is too late for that.

"Somewhere like this place," I say to my husband. "It's nice here."

"It is," he says. "And far and foreign, miles away from anything."

"Isn't that a good thing?"

"It's good if that's what a person wants."

"I just want to go home," I say.

The bus drops us back at the hotel with an hour to spare before dinner. Julian wants his evening swim but there isn't time and the pain in my back has tired me out.

"Just a quick one," he says.

"Then straight to dinner," I say.

"Yes, Mother," he says.

"I'm warning you," I say, wagging my finger at him.

"Come rest your back," Mark says.

We have emerged from the desert into an oasis, the bed made, the room warm from the day and with the glass doors closed the quiet is soothing. My husband says that one good thing about this place is the abundance of fish, he's never eaten so much fish in his life. I say I'd be happy never to leave this room, ever, to lie here, the sea and traffic humming beyond the glass, the rustling of pages as he reads his book.

"I want them to move Julian closer," I say.

"We can ask."

"Or we could move to that end of the passage," I say.

"What are you worried about?"

"About Julian," I say.

"He can look after himself," he says.

"No, he can't," I say. "He's fifteen."

"Jesus, Claude," he says. "I was having sex at his age."

"And?" I say. "So was I."

"No, you weren't," he says.

"Can you just call them?" I say. "Tell them we want to move."

"At fifteen?" he says. "Really?"

"Do you notice how men look at him?" I say.

"What do you mean?"

"That man in the pool in the evenings. He stares at Julian."

"He's a good-looking boy."

"Exactly," I say. "A boy."

It happened just that once, and for a long time after that never again with anyone.

"That guy who eats alone," I say.

"Which one?"

My husband is not the most perceptive. When it's dinner time he's focused on his dinner. I know he's trying not to make a fuss, as if he can't see what has happened, this burning down of the business, the shop, the machines, computers, desks, the new chairs we'd bought a couple of weeks ago.

"He's got a dirty-old-man look," I say.

"If he's old," Mark says. "What would you call me?"

"What's a man doing alone in a place like this?"

"Let's ask him," he says.

"Don't," I say.

"He doesn't look like a paedophile," Mark says.

"What does that mean?"

"He doesn't look like he'd make a pass at Julian," he says. "Like he'd touch him."

"I can't listen to this," I say. "This is obscene."

The next morning at breakfast, walking with our plates from the buffet, my husband stops at the man's table.

"Can we join you?" he says.

"Of course," the man says.

He's French. His dark hair brushes against his shoulders when he glances around the room, bemused, there are many empty tables. Still, he moves his plate of toast and a small jug of milk to make room for us.

"Only the two of you?" he says.

"What do you mean?" I say.

"Your son?"

"The lazy teenager," my husband says.

"They need to sleep," the man says. "Growing pains."

"He's grown enough," I say.

"Have you hurt your back?"

"It comes and goes," I say, my gaze fixed on my plate, the scrambled eggs, the rinds of bacon.

Jean-Luc is an acupuncturist and masseur, he comes to Spain a couple of times a year to see clients at a local clinic. He tells us his son will be arriving from Lyon later that morning, he's collecting him from the airport. This is their holiday time together.

"We'll be home by Friday," I say. "I've already booked a session."

"It's no problem," he says. "I am happy to see you."

"Go," my husband says. "We've got a packed flight ahead of us."

"Fine," I say. "But no needles."

Our son stands at our table smiling down at us, and

the man smiles up at him.

"The lazy son," my husband says.

Julian holds out his hand to the man and says, "Hey, Jean-Luc."

"You ready for a rematch, young man?"

Later that afternoon, when my husband and I meet Jean-Luc in the indoor pool area, there's a boy strapped to a high-backed wheelchair facing the pool. His eyes shift when we come into his field of vision. The place is hot and humid, and the sun comes in through the glass walls.

"Would you mind keeping an eye on Serge?" Jean-Luc says to my husband.

"Sure," Mark says.

"He likes being read to," Jean-Luc says.

"Does he speak English?" I say.

"No," Jean-Luc smiles. "But he likes to listen."

"Detective novels?" Mark says to the boy. "*Romans policiers?*"

The boy smiles at him, his mouth full of teeth.

Jean-Luc and I go up in the lift together, not completely like strangers, even though this is the first time we're alone together. He makes light conversation, asks how long I've been seeing my massage therapist, if I've ever had my back X-rayed. My answers are abrupt, they taste like accusations. I don't ask about his son, about the boy's mother. A handsome boy with a healthy head of hair, blue eyes, a version of his father, misaligned.

When we enter the room, Jean-Luc's voice becomes soft. The lights have been dimmed and the curtains are closed despite us being too high up for anyone to see in. The massage table is set up between his bed and the desk. Jean-Luc turns to light a candle and switches on some music, a sitar, the soft drumming of the tabla.

"Whatever is comfortable for you," he says.

So I remove my clothes, my underwear, and climb onto the table while his gaze is averted. The towel he uses is warm against my back and buttocks, and he presses his palms into my shoulders, and down, peels the towel to one side and moves to my legs, my shins and calves and with warmed oil kneads my skin upwards, releasing everything. He is firm and confident, and all the while I can feel his eyes on me, my legs, my back, his hands in constant motion, the soft strings of the sitar, the drumming of fingertips, and because I cannot move and I have chosen to be here, the only option I have is to surrender to his touch.

Not Alone Enough

1 According to the guidebook the cemetery is Hackney's oasis, no other burial ground is better served in English Literature. This is the resting place of William Booth, father of the Salvation Army. It's a refuge for the drunk, a haven for school children and couples in love. I am here at the far end, on a bench by the path that flanks Bouverie Road. Over the high wall, I can see the nursery school where I used to work (for a couple of years, I was the lunchtime cook).

The sun filters through the leaves and turns the tree-tops into lace. The grave beside me has a bunch of everlasting poppies on it. A man in denim cut-offs and flip-flops is coming towards me, reading a book as he walks. I'm set with new expectations. He stops and the tension mounts, his well-trained eye sizes me up. When he pauses I am transformed, reshaped by desire and shame. I cling like Jacob to Esau's ankle, hauled from place to place.

"Have you got the time?" he says.

Clichés that invite possibilities. I could tell him the story of Jung in Morocco and how he'd fumble for his pocket-watch each time he saw pretty boys on beaches or in the Atlas Mountains.

"Around noon," I say.

2. Envy says: I want to be you.

3. Something to look into: I am Hephaestus, the foot-dragging maker-of-arms. The mountain from which I am thrown, a triangle, in need of sharp corners. Approaching the end of my myth, I'll need to start making choices.

4. Last night at a poet's party I got drunk on chilled rosé and begged a man in a terra cotta T-shirt to have sex with me. From what I can remember, I said things like: I can tell by your beauty that you're a poet, well-versed in pain. You know your metaphors. He laughed and fed me smoked salmon sandwiches to sober me up. I said I'd kiss him right there and then. I said: These cocktail parties make me want to have wild, desperate sex. I don't care if everyone sees me naked.

"I'm not gay," he said.

"No one's perfect," I said.

5. Tell me this: What made Daedalus fly in front of his

son and not behind him, like a good father should. Let's face it, you can't keep an eye on your boy if he's not in your field of vision. There are consequences to that sort of behaviour. Daedalus rebuilt his life after Icarus' death, the rest of his days spent in mourning, sick with guilt.

6. What I'm going to tell you might shock you. I took the guy home from the cemetery and he swallowed my fist up his arse. Poppers would have made it easier, he said, but he needed it too much to care. He'd sat down on the bench beside me, feigning interest in my notebook, telling me how he'd always wanted to be a writer. He was sweaty from walking around the cemetery for hours.

"It's hot," I said.

"Can you make me hotter?" he said, tucking his hand under my notebook.

He cupped me in his fist and smiled.

"It's not that big," I said.

"Big enough," he said. "Follow me into the bushes."

"I live just down the road," I said.

"But I don't know you," he said.

"It's just sex," I said. "It's not like I'm going to kill you."

We left the cemetery laughing, holding hands as if we were lovers already. We bought apple juice from Harvest Wines and fat purple grapes from the grocers by the funeral parlour. By the time we got home I knew everything I'd ever know about him, except one story. He told me enough names, dates and places to explain how he could lie back on a stranger's bed, stretch open his arse and say: Look, just like a pussy.

7. I had a German lover who brought pastures and farmhouses to our relationship. He was as beautiful as the young Chekhov, taller, equally insatiable. I'd met Rudolph on a sofa in the foyer of the National Gallery under the painting of the Battle of Waterloo. His body promised protection, his worldliness offered riches. A diplomat, he made me tie him up while I spoke to friends on the phone. I was danger and exotica to him. He'd never been in love with a Jew. He taught me that men love to get fucked, to disappear, to be ripped open. I tell you this in case you're wondering how it all started.

8. In the silence after we came, I stroked the down on the cheeks of his arse, ran the tips of my fingers along his spine, put my arm across his shoulder, the arm that had been inside him, my elbow nestling in the curve of his neck. I touched his face as if it were a baby's.

"Are you working tomorrow?" I said.

"I must go home soon," he said.

"You can stay if you like."

"I need to go," he said. "It doesn't mean I won't see you again."

The sweat dried on my skin and I pulled the duvet up from the foot of the bed. He wrote his name and number on a piece of paper; I said what I said, and he told me one last story.

9. Wherever I go, I'm there to find love. The guidebook says that in spring and early summer, a rich variety of bird-song adds to the idyllic woodland aura. It's true for mid-summer, too: the woodland aura is idyllic. My task for the day is compassion. Two bodies: one standing to comfort the one who kneels, weeping. The comforter holds the weeping man's head in his hands, caresses his hair, his nape, the outline of his shoulders. The man in tears leans his head into the other man's body, and no matter how hard I try, I can't stop him from sucking the other guy's cock.

10. Creativity is trickery. Pretend to know everything, pretend to belong, pretend our stories mean something to the world, even if the world is just one person.

11. "Talk to me. Stop ignoring me."
    "I'm sorry," I say. "Not right now."

12. I couldn't face the cemetery this morning, don't ask me why, so I went to the café in Clissold Park. The sun had emancipated the privileged of Stoke Newington,

those who don't have or need jobs, and the lawn is bustling with mothers and children, men playing chess with their shirts off, one with a guitar in his lap. I sit on the stairs outside with a mug of Earl Grey tea. Gisi sees me and comes over. She says she misses the coffee houses in Berlin.

"I just love all this green," I say. "Half my life I've lived in the desert."

Other mothers join us with their children. A year since I left my job at the nursery school. Why did I leave? I couldn't stop remembering my own childhood. To love children you must believe in a future, you can't be bound to your own messy past and care for children at the same time. Every loving gesture is an attempt to remedy my own sadness.

Later, back in the cemetery, behind the derelict chapel, there's a patch of grass with a bench. This is tranquillity. Then a man sits down in front of me, removes his shoes and shirt. An onion-skin of sweat covers his body, his nipples are dark brown. I can't imagine doing anything gentle to him. Shame was born in the footsteps of love. Shame and fear turn compassion into cruelty. I want trees and grass and silence. I want the sun to myself. I look up and my eyes are open palms. Look away and I am shame. So, if I talk to him, what will happen? We'll head off into the trees, and there amongst the tombstones and fern bushes and clinging ivy, before we kiss, before we taste each other, before we learn too much about one another from the way we touch, he'll put his hand up my shirt and recoil from my body.

Wait.

A story's about to unfold. A real-life, juicy, flesh-and-fucking story is about to make its debut on the arena. The man with the porn-star's body walks across the path with his T-shirt tucked into his back pocket. The bulk of his cock has left a permanent outline on the fabric of his jeans. Skin browned from being half-naked wherever he goes – walking home from the gym, sitting on an old chair in his back garden, cruising the cemetery to make sure everyone has had a taste of him.

I'll do anything to be next.

My notebook morphs into a psalter as I slide off the bench onto my knees. Put him into words, imprint every pore and hair of his body onto yours. Record everything, note the way he smoothes his palm across his chest, the way his nipples darken like an invitation as the chapel's stained glass windows begin to crack and crash to the ground. The choir is singing deafening hosannas as Jesus howls and rips rusting nails from his aching flesh. Ecstasy is loosed upon the world, brothers. This, at some point, will be the opening scene of something.

13. The porn-star settles down on a tombstone by the tap near the main path, lights a cigarette. I can tell he's a

regular in this place, the kind of man who can pick and choose. Men with bodies like his can mask their inner world with greater ease. Confession is not a prerequisite for affection. Does he know I can bring him voluptuous pleasure? Is he aware of the wondrous things I've done with my penis? Joy is born with the words I and love and you stringed together. Joy revels in its own being, untangled from memory. Wait, there's more. The porn-star runs cool water into his open palm and splashes water into his hair. The strip of sun between the chapel and tree-tops has narrowed into an aisle for him to walk down, naked, velvet skin exposed and welcoming.

14. Desire risks being torn to pieces. This is where Hephaestus comes back into the story. No matter how hard his father kicks him, he accepts his mother's call to move back in. The next few years he spends at home, albeit on Mount Olympus, making weapons for the gods, helping others fight their battles. Desire closes down the mind in order to survive. You're the first person I'm telling this to. Do you want to know what happened three days ago? I met this man in the cemetery and I fell in love. Maybe you're wondering: a) How long does it take one to fall in love? and b) How can you love someone you don't even know? And the answers: a) Time's not a factor, and b) You've not been in love much, have you?

15. What about last week's cemetery-man with the book? What was the story he told you? He handed me that slip of paper with his name and number, and I'm like: That's a nice Jewish name. So he tells me about his grandparents and their travelling theatre company.

We're talking 1930s and 40s. They're Germans, and when the war starts they join the Nazi party, which means they got invited to perform for SS officers. They travel between concentration camps performing Schiller, but when they realise what's going on beyond the officers' quarters, they begin to hide Jews and Gypsies amongst the costumes in their caravans and drive them out to the partisans in the woods.

But that was then, and this is now: The porn-star's name is Henrik and turns out he's Denmark's number one rock star, 6'2" with jet-black hair, here in London for the kind of sex he likes. This is what I can tell you about him: He smiles openly and walks as if he's never been lost. While I'm on my knees before him, he leans against the chapel wall, his middle damp with sweat and someone else's smell. He dribbles spit down at me, so I can wet my lips, says he wants to be taken out in the open. The possibility of discovery turns him on. While I'm inside him, watching myself go in and out, I ask him questions and he tells me things. That's what makes me love him, he knew I could be trusted. By the time we're finished, the cemetery gates are locked, so we climb through a hole in the fence by the timber yard and go for drinks at Bar Lorca.

"I'm going to be in *Hamlet*, the musical," he says.

"Are you Hamlet?" I say.

"Yes," he says. "What do you do?" (Hadn't I told him already?)

"I'm a writer," I say.

"I write sometimes," he says. "After two or three days writing, when I go out again, I feel like the loneliest man in the world."

"That's me most days," I say.

When they call for last drinks I suggest we go for coffee, and each time he agrees I feel braver, a god-fearing Christian in the lion's den, charming the beast with divine reassurance. We buy coffee at the kebab place and walk down Church Street, stopping to look at children's clothes in the window of a second-hand shop. He leans in towards me, thinking I want to whisper in his ear, me thinking he wants a kiss.

"I don't think I can return that," he says.

"I thought not," I say, claw-marks across my cheek.

"You're not looking for quick sex," he says. "You're looking for love."

He left without giving me his phone number, but I'm a Rottweiler when it comes to love. A few days later, I ask the Danish Tourist Board to send me information about musicals in Copenhagen. On the day of the première I send him flowers with a postcard of a stone angel on one of the tombstones in Abney Park Cemetery. A call comes two days later.

"Thank you for the flowers," he says.

"Do you like them?" I say.

"Can I see you when I come to London?"

Every heartbeat threatens to take it all away.

16. I want to make every entrance with glee. Blindly, hopefully, ready for everything. So what if I'm drunk? I'm in love. Twice in one month is not a lot compared to adolescence. But you're thirty-five. No, I'm not. I'm five, sometimes fifteen, never more. Falling in love is addictive. All that promise. All that license for abandon and danger, or is it an addiction to the pain of disappointment? It's too cold for the cemetery, I'm going down to the river.

Walking through Covent Garden on the way to the South Bank I stop at Tesco's for a tub of humous and two ciabatta rolls. I cross Hungerford Bridge and walk along the river to Gabriel's Wharf where a festival of street performers is in full swing. I lean against the railings and watch a young man in a kilt balance on the handlebars of his BMX. He jumps from one side of his bike to the other, like some cowboy acrobat, his kilt exposing Hello Kitty boxer shorts whenever his legs are in the air.

"This is my only job," he tells his audience before his

last trick. "So if you like the show, please support it. And if you can't spare a pound, come up and say hi."

"Can I buy you a drink?" I say.

"You sure can," he says. "My fucking girlfriend didn't turn up and I'm vexed."

Ripples lap against the embankment wall, echoes of waves crashing on African shores. On a day like today Icarus drowned, and as his body sunk down to the ocean floor, there was Hephaestus and a bunch of nymphs making bracelets and friendship rings.

"I don't like my lovers to see what I do," I say.

"I don't love her," he says. "Besides, I need to be looked at."

"I'll look at you."

"Let's drink, then," he says.

17. Who gave birth to detachment? Pain. And pain? A slap in the face. Detachment is eyes rolled back, seeing nothing, not even its own insides. The weather's improved. I'm on a bench in the cemetery again. I convince myself of this: I'm here to explore. I've given up on love. All I want is to survive these days. Biker-boy had followed me home from the river and asked me to tie him to my bed, but futons are problematic when it comes to bondage, so I strapped his wrists to my writing desk, lifted his legs over my shoulders. He kept telling me to do it harder, getting louder and louder, until he said: "Did

you come already?"

And I, pulling out of him, ejaculated into my hand, offered it to him. He wiggled his tongue over my open palm, as if it were boiling water, saying: "God, I'd love to swallow it," until he came, too. I wiped his cum off my thigh with a tissue. We don't share smiles, just the sheer exhilaration of disgust. Humiliation is on the floor. Head in palms, heart against knees, exposing buttocks and spine. Humiliation couldn't give a fuck. Protect me, violate me, whatever, as long as I don't have to open my eyes.

18. That was Sunday, now it's Friday, and this little boy with black-rimmed glasses waddles up to the bench and sits down beside me. His striped T-shirt hugs his body and his red shorts cling to his thighs. He tries to hold my hand, fingers sweaty against mine. I show him the bit in the guidebook where it says there's a strong educational aspect to the cemetery.

"The trees and shrubs," I tell him, "are labelled for the enlightenment of all who visit?"

"Hug me," he says.

"Where's your mummy?" I say.

"I'm with *you*," he says.

"Who's looking after you?" I say.

"You are," he says.

"I'm not looking after you, silly."

"Yes, you are."

"I don't even know your name," I say.

He covers his face with his hands and peeps at me through his fingers.

"Yes, you do, silly" he says.

But suddenly he freezes, his eyes dart past me. A man and a woman are coming up the path. I figure they must be his parents, but when I turn to ask him the bench is empty. The man's looking into the trees and reading tombstones. The woman says: "First we'll need to put in a rod to check how deep the grave is. I want to make sure there's room for you." The price depends on how far the grave is from the footpath: if it's too far they'll need to dig by hand. That'll cost anywhere up to £500. He tells the woman that money isn't a factor, that he wants to be buried with his mother. They walk off down a side path and the boy returns.

"Have they gone?"

"Who?" I say.

"Those people."

"Who are they?" I say.

"He looked scary," says the boy.

"Do you know where you live?" I say.

"97 Pallatine Road, silly," he says.

He takes my hand and drapes it across his shoulder, leans into my armpit, fits his body into mine.

"You never play with me anymore," he says.

"What should we play?"

"Hide 'n' seek," he says. "And you're *it*."

But we sit in silence, his head on my shoulder, me peering over the top of his head breathing in the scent of Johnson's Baby Shampoo. A man in lycra shorts jogs past, rucksack on his back. A couple stands at the edge of the path, unsure which way to turn, their conversation animated: "I hadn't spoken to her in *seven* years, and then there she was, on the phone, babbling on about some wedding she was off to in Scotland." Another man appears from the opposite end of the path on his bicycle. A great sense of elation as he slows down, dismounts, comes closer, a blond angel with a sprinkling of light brown hair on his chest. I walk towards him, my mouth dry from fear my voice will squeak. I keep all sounds in the back of my throat: "Hi." And he says: "Hi." And I say: "What are you doing?" And he says: "Cycling. You?"

"Not much," I say. "Just writing."

While we stand there talking, he dislodges himself from his shorts, a finger puppet, squeezing the pink head out of its sheath, coaxing it.

"This way," he says, and leads me into the bushes, propping his bike up against a tree.

His eyes are blue, his skin taut. His lips are soft and the noises he makes are the sound of unexpected and accurate pleasuring, the sound one makes when one is happy to be weak and vulnerable. We are strangers in a forest jerking each other off. He whispers things into my mouth like: Can I see you again? You're hot. We smile at each other. I tell him to keep flicking my nipples like that until it's all over.

"Where have you been?" the boy says.

"Here," I say.

"I thought you'd forgotten me. Did you go away to another country?"

"No, I was here," I say.

"Can we go and play now?"

He takes my hand and we walk through the cemetery. He waves to the drunks who wave back, calling his name. He runs up to the bench where they're sitting and snuggles in between them, a big grin on his face, ready to have his picture taken. They offer him sweets, stroke his brown hair. He joins a group of school children gathering pebbles, and I watch the breeze flips leaves across the path, change them from emerald to dusty green. The boy wanders into the ruined chapel, then immediately runs back out, giggling. He grips my leg and I ruffle his hair: Let's walk down there towards the exit. I slip my notebook into my pocket and pick him up as we amble amongst the trees back out onto the main path. This is a picture of glee. I say to him: Are you ready? as I lift him from under his arms and throw him into the air. The sky is blue behind him, the clouds unmarked by grey. He

falls back into my arms, shrieking.
    "Again," he says.

Abney Park Cemetery, Stoke Newington, 2005

The Smell of Asparagus Pee

My sweetness, I am writing to you because only you understand me, only you know I am worth loving. If I tell you I'm going mad, you won't run away. If I tell you I've often felt like killing myself – a craft knife to my wrists, the front of the Victoria Line to Brixton – you hold me and listen to the details of my plan, ask questions where appropriate, encourage me to tell you everything. You don't try to calm or cure me or tell me stories about those who rescued themselves from despair, others who could not and in the end killed themselves. You never say: You're not like them, like the ones who did. You've got so much going for you.

I'm writing to you because you think I'm wonderful. You think I'm sexy. You think my love handles are really love handles and not handfuls of flesh. You think the hair on my back is soft and silky, the most gorgeous thing to rest your head on, run the tips of your fingers along, and sometimes you stroke my back, no, *often* you stroke my back while I'm asleep and I open my eyes to see you propped up on your elbow staring at me as if I were your own creation, the person you've been waiting for all your life.

You've loved me from the day we met and you've never stopped loving me since. Sweetness, how long has it been since we met? Is it years or months? Years, I'm telling you. We've been together for years and you've seen me at my worst and at my best and even when I'm at my best you know it's elusive, fleeting, because by the time we get home – from the book launch, the cocktail party, the club where we've been dancing so beautifully all night – by the time we get home I'm tearing chunks of hair from my scalp and lashing out at you. But you hold me and let me wail until I'm tired and curl up asleep in your arms. And when I awake, there you are, holding me, saying: I'm with you. Should I get us some tea?

I'm writing to ask you to come home. I can't stand being on my own any longer, sleeping alone in our bed. You're the only one in whose arms I can sleep. I've told you that, to your face and in all the letters I've sent. When I sleep, I need your arms around me. I'm writing because you said I could. You said: Write letters and tell me everything, every detail of your days: what you're doing, thinking, all the letters you've written, every phone-call you've made, the weather, how the garden's doing (are the daffodils and hyacinths out yet? Is the back wall covered in ivy?). You said: Tell me what the neighbours have been up to, what you paid for the sweet potatoes and crisp red apples. Tell me all the things you wanted to do but didn't. Those things. Everything. I want to know everything. So this is it, sweetness, I'm writing to tell you everything.

I'm writing to tell you that I went to the post office today to send a story to Canada. I'm going to be in an anthology there. They love my work. Just like you, sweetness. The editor said my story's exactly what she's looking for. The man at the post office, Bash, recognised me and smiled and said: Alright? and offered me a sample carton of Fruit Bix, but I couldn't bear to be seen taking anything from anyone, the indignity of having my needs witnessed. It's enough I have to write these letters to you. I will not go down on my knees in a public place and say: Please. Then I went to the grocers for broccoli for my pasta and tuna bake. Also: an iceberg lettuce, carrots, lemons (they're still 3 for 60p). Is that what you mean, sweetness? Is that what you mean when you say: Tell me everything?

I'm writing to tell you that the thyme and oregano are doing well after the winter. I need herbs for my pasta bake, and that's why I'm telling you this. Everything has a reason, sweetness, I'm not babbling. I'm telling you this because a) you asked me to, and b) herbs are a part of my life. I have grown them out of nothing. And I have fought to keep them alive. The snails still leave slime trails on the oregano leaves turning them silver when they catch the light. The rosemary's flowering for the first time, and the daffodils outside our bedroom window have begun to appear. They should be out in a week or two if you want to make sure you're here before they bloom.

I'm writing to tell you... Can I tell you this? Can I tell you that I'm waiting for someone? I'm waiting for a man I slept with two weeks ago to come and be with me. Can I tell you that someone is coming to sleep with me tonight, sweetness? He's late, and I'm doing all the regular things, pacing up and down, staring at the phone, thinking: Ring! Ring! Preparing food and telling myself it's for me, to last for the next few days, not made especially for the coming of this man. And what if he doesn't come, what am I supposed to do then, sweetness? How do I go on if he doesn't turn up and you aren't here and I have to spend one more night in our bed alone?

I'm writing to tell you this: I don't know if I can bear another night on my own. It's been months since you were last here in bed with me. No, years, it's been years since you slept with me, since you let me make love to you and pound you with all my envy and self-hatred, and you took everything. You did. You tried to make the horror go away. You still do. You say to me: Nothing you say scares me. Nothing you say will be too terrible.

I love you.

I'm writing to you because I don't have anyone to talk to. I don't have friends I can call on the phone and say: Let's go for a pizza. Let's have fun, talk about feelings. I don't have friends in faraway places, safely distant from here, ones I can write to, ones who talk depression with analytical skill. I used to have many friends, but there comes a time in each friendship when everything becomes unbearable and I have to move away or push them away or else I land up not having anything to give and then I have to say: We have nothing in common. And they're hurt and stunned and sometimes they cry. They do. I've made people cry when I tell them about my feelings. My world upsets people. Remember the therapist who cried when I read her a friend's letter to me?

What's going on, sweetness. What's happening? Can you see I'm going mad? I can't stop myself. I can't. I'm like a virus, a cancer, a bull in a china shop. Help me, sweetness. The men I love can never love me. I choose them with that in mind. You know about them, about David, my nursery-school love, who taught me to hunt for snakes behind Mr Faber's toy shop, steal fire-crackers from the Greek grocers. You know about Simon who visited me on the farm up north and slept in white briefs on a mattress on the floor, and me, emboldened by the agony of lust, invited him to sleep in my bed.

Poor Simon, flustered, fiddling with his earphones, saying: You can borrow my Walkman if you like, it's Stevie Wonder. But you're different, sweetness. Thank God. You're the first man I've ever loved who has loved me back. With all your heart. I frighten men with my wholeheartedness. Men know my love is not a joyous one. No fun and games here.

Men love selfish lovers. They love to fight for their love, feel the pain of one-sided love. They love to feel chivalrous and denied and heartbroken. So who's going to write the book about men who love too much? Who'll make the film about men on the verge of a nervous breakdown? Who'll stand up and say: There are men in this world who enjoy the voluptuous pain of love. Who will admit that men hate selfless lovers unless all they want is to be fucked, humiliated and beaten up? You see, sweetness, I'm all of the above. Wholeheartedly. And that's why a) you love me and b) it's always easy to find a man to fuck.

I am writing to you because I need you to hold my hand, sweetness. Cradle and hug me and hold me and tell me exactly what I want to hear. Be here with me, sweetness. Your body and your arms and your chest and your willingness to take all of me into you and just hold me and rock me and kiss my eyelids and press your forehead against mine and rub my back and my bum and gently, gently use your wet finger as if I were a baby, teething.

Oh, sweetness, I need you to help me sleep. Don't you know all this already? Don't you know? So why aren't you here with me? Why don't you pack your bags and make your way home? I keep telling you everything, just like you asked, and still you're so far away. I gave you a point by point account in my last letter of the preceding months. I thought: The more I tell him the more he'll know, and the more he knows the more likely he is to come home. Things like: Thursday 21 October: 1) I am woken by my cold feet peeping out the end of the duvet. 2) I don't wake with hard-ons anymore. 3) I don't need to piss. 4) I lie with your teddy on my chest. And 5) Teddy misses you. Three thousand points in one letter. Thank God my memory's photographic. Thank God I remember everything exactly how it happened. I showed the letter to Pauline before I sent it and she said: Wouldn't it be easier if your sweetness had a phone in that posh house of his? She said: You didn't do that, you never told me about that, and who the fuck is Henry?

I am writing to tell you about Henry, sweetness. Do you really want to know? Can't we keep Henry for a separate letter. Let's put Henry on the back-burner and eat him later. I'm writing to you because this could be a story. You see, if I fictionalise my life or at least get a story out of it and make some money then I can believe it's all worth it. But when no story comes and even when it does and no-one wants it, then everything is death.

Meaning, life, food, love. Pointless. You know what it's like, sweetness, hours spent creating stories and then people say no. I show them my life and they say: I'm not sure we could publish that. Sorry, that's not quite for us. In real life it's the same, because he still hasn't called and still hasn't turned up. Why do people do that, sweetness? Do you think it's okay for someone you've slept with not to call. All that intimacy and then he's running away. And he'd said: I'll let you know when I'm on my way.

I'm writing to tell you I'm physically and emotionally famished. I can't wait for him any longer. Him, that is, the man who's supposed to be here. No, not Henry. I said we'd leave him for later. You don't want the details, believe me. There's this other man who I can't wait for, so I'm going to eat the tuna, broccoli, peas and pasta bake I made with freshly ground nutmeg, lots of black pepper, served with a vinaigrette salad. Are you thinking: It's been years since he cooked for me, months since we ate together and he surprised me with fresh asparagus and hollandaise sauce. Remember that first time you smelt your asparagus pee? You couldn't believe something so foul could come from you. I'm used to such smells, revolting odours, I've smelt my sewers, so the smell of asparagus pee has always been a relief, to know exactly from whence cometh the putrid stink.

I'm not a good cook anymore. I used to be. I don't

want to cook for myself. I don't want to cook potfuls of bolognese or mashed potato with mango pickle and garam masala (you haven't tasted that dish yet, have you?). I hate cooking huge pots of food and having to eat the same thing for days in a row. I can't cook for one person. I've never be able to. What a waste to cook for one. Food should never be prepared like that. So now I cook less and I forget, so I need to go back to recipe books. There's another man coming to be with me (or at least I thought there was) and I've been cooking, a pasta bake, which I've eaten most of and which, admittedly, lacks oomph, no chewy bits, nothing to get your teeth into, no chunks of Italian sausage, no mushrooms. None of that. And for dessert: Rum and raisin chocolate-chip cookies and a mug of rooibos tea.

I'm writing to tell you that I made chocolate-chip cookies for this man who says he's on his way. Should I tell you his name? Should I, like you say, tell you everything? Will that bring you back? If you can imagine him, name and all, if I give you a detailed description will that bring you home? Will jealousy bring you back? Will the unbearable thought of me making love to another man bring you to me? You don't believe me, do you? You don't think I've got the guts to be with another man. You think that because I trusted you I'll never be able to trust another man, that because I gave all my trust I'm left with nothing. But this man lets me fuck him, sweetness, which is how it all started, you see. We'd hardly said two words to each other and he was dragging me home, pulling down his trousers, handing me a tube of KY and a condom, and saying: There, fuck it.

His name is. His name is. I can't. I can't say his name, although I've told Pauline about him. She hasn't met him, because we're still at the keeping-him-to-myself stage, that stage of togetherness where things are still symbiotic and infantile. Tell me what you're doing, sweetness. Tell me what you're doing while you read this letter. I imagine you pacing a long porch wrapped around a house with wicker armchairs and bright Georgia O'Keeffe cushions. It's like a scene from a movie I saw years ago about a group of women who cut off their tongues. Was it in Maine, in one of those old houses overlooking the sea? I imagine you in a landscape like that. Big trees and green lawns and lots of sunlight and you on the porch, alone, because you want to be alone, and you can, because the house belongs to someone you know and they're letting you stay there. They know you need this time to yourself. Time away from me.

You said you wouldn't be gone for long, and it's been years now, sweetness. No, months, it's been months since you left. I can't imagine what a year would look like when every moment is a nightmare. I can't imagine what so many of these joined together would look like. I can't bear having to curl up into a foetus for hours to take the pain away. To forget myself. It's a coping mechanism: revert to foetushood. That and getting drunk and smoking weed and walking for hours and ploughing through Chekhov.

I'm writing to tell you to read "Man in a Case," "Gooseberries," and "Concerning Love." They are my coping mechanisms. Chekhov rescues me. Friendship stories make me hopeful. I read about Alyokhin washing himself in the bathing-hut, chatting to Burkin, and Ivan Ivanovich diving in and out of the pool as the water-lilies bob around him, saying: "Oh, God, oh dear God," because there are no words to describe the delight of swimming in the rain with friends on a warm day.

The more I miss you the harder it gets to be with anyone else. Ah, you say, but what about this man you're waiting for? This man you've made pasta for? This man you've baked cookies for? What about him? (And Henry?) But this man lets me fuck him, sweetness. That's all he wants. We don't talk because we have nothing to say, no matter how hard we try. Should I tell you more about him. His name is. I see you jumping up, slamming the letter onto the coffee table and saying: Jesus Christ, tell me his fucking name already. Get it over with.

He's a beautiful man with long thin fingers, artist's fingers, because he's a painter, and he has narrow hips and broad shoulders and a bit of a belly that's like baby fat, and he doesn't talk much about his feelings and he gets defensive, but when I ignore him he nuzzles up to me and sniffs my armpit and licks my hand and my God is he beautiful. His tight curls are cropped close to his skull and his skin is so smooth that sometimes when I hold him and close my eyes and stroke his back and his bum I am with a woman. He hardly sweats and he doesn't have body odour even if he's been painting all day, even then he only smells of paint and turps and his special tea-tree soap. He never calls me anything and I call him Sweetness, only because I miss you, and every man I sleep with I call Sweetness because then I can trick myself into thinking they're you. Everyone is you, sweetness. Everything is you.

There's a pile of letters on the stairs addressed to you. I'll keep them here for when you come home. All sorts of bills, which I've paid (don't ask me how), six letters from your mother, who is frantic and keeps demanding that you write and tell her what's happening. She wants to know where you were for Christmas. I keep expecting her to turn up on our doorstep. Every knock on the door could be her. Luckily she doesn't have our new phone number. Did I tell you we're ex-directory and known only to a chosen few? I imagine her climbing the stairs to our front door and me having to speak to her. Where's my son, she'll say. Where is he? And she'll push me aside and position herself, limbs akimbo in the living room, saying: What's this mess, where's all the furniture and who the fuck are you?

I'm going to tell your mother that you were here for Christmas. It was definitely this Christmas we spent together, just the two of us, no guests, no rushing off to be elsewhere. We didn't have a tree or decorations, but I cooked whatever Christians cook for Christmas. I'll say to her: Has he told you about my cooking, because he's told me about yours. And she'll say, because I know the kind of woman she is, she'll say: I don't give a fuck about your cooking. Where's my son? What have you done with my son?

If your mother turns up, I'll tell her everything. I will not lie. I'm going to tell her that we've loved each other for years, from the second we met, and then I'm going to tell her where we met, when we met, and exactly what we've been doing from that moment on. She needs to know if she wants to know. Mothers deserve the truth. This is not a threat, sweetness. I don't want it to sound like a threat. I'm desperate. This is what begging sounds like. This is what a demented person sick with love sounds like. Please come home. How can you stay away for so long if you love me so much? I know you do. I know you love me from the way you held me the night before you left. You told me you'd be back as soon as you'd sorted things out. There was so much you needed to do. All these things going on in your head and you had people to see in America and we could both do with a break after all these years cooped up inside. See, it is years. I'm not going mad and imagining things. We've been together for years. Have you seen them by now, have you spoken to all those people in America?

I often think about our last night together. I can still smell you in the house. I see the shape of your body in the sofa cushions, feel you in our bed, even if there's going to be another man in there tonight. And if not him I'll be too crazed to spend another night on my own and I'll go out and return with someone new. Men like deranged skinny men who want to fuck them. I can do that for them. I cannot fuck with love. I fuck with anger and, believe me, since I've discovered anger it's opened up a whole new world. Men love to be fucked with anger. They just lie back and enjoy themselves.

I'm going on and on, aren't I, sweetness? Have you nodded off there on your porch amongst women who crop their tongues out and chop off their breasts? Or are you reading this and thinking: God, I miss him and that intensity. Are you saying (is there someone there to say this to, a well-dressed American: a Gertrude Steinian? a Capote lookalikeian?) are you saying: I need to get everything packed and book a flight to London. Have you looked up every now and then to let your mind wander because I've reminded you of something precious? Because we do have good memories. Do you need me to refresh your memory. I like that: Refresh your memory.

I'll make your memory fresh: us on the beach, that summer morning with no one around, me and you rolling in the sand like biscuits in sugar, covering ourselves, our hair and ears, sand in our swimming trunks, which you were too shy to take off. Then we ran into the water and back onto the shore to roll about again, and you said: We're like a pair of dogs in dirt.

That was the day I taught you to eat food off our bodies, to squash fresh strawberries against my arse and lap them up, spread warm chocolate on your chest and jerk yourself off and only then would I kneel beside you with a spoon. My precious pudding. My chocolate-spread memory. My distant kiss. My faraway fuck. My thorn in the throat. How could you leave me how could you how could you how could you. I could go on like that forever, getting my fingers caught in that rhythm on the keyboards: How could you. How could you. How could you. Numb the words into nothingness through repetition. How could you how could you. It has a beat to it. How could you. How could you.

Okay. Okay. No more memories. I'll tell you everything about now. I'll tell you what I'm doing. Well, I'm writing a letter and waiting. No, he's not the same man. This is a new day and there's another man. This one is different. This one is dying and he's coming for dinner. He's coming to eat the tuna and pasta bake that wasn't appreciated yesterday. This man will approve of the dish. He loves everything I make. He looks at me and I can see the love in his eyes. But you are the only one I can ever love back. Only you look at me with love and I am grateful. Other people's love scares me. They want things, expect me to love them back. That scares me and then my contempt for them becomes a wall between us. With you it's different. You are my one true love.

This man's name is Henry. He is much younger than me and he thinks I'm gorgeous. No, not the Henry you know. That Henry is old. My Henry is from the new generation of Henrys, names that skip a generation, so you can imagine how young he is, two generations away from us. This Henry came up to me after a reading and asked if he could buy me a drink. Don't raise your eyebrows like that. The youngsters of today take risks. They do. Henry takes risks. He'll do anything to get what he wants. He's fearless. In his twenty-two years, he's been through more than we'll ever go through. Nine brothers and sisters, poverty, foster homes, sexual abuse, prostitution, rape, shit jobs. Now he lives from hand to mouth and drinks as much as he can.

I know I said I'd leave the details for another letter, and I know this is going to hurt you. I know you want to be my one and only. I'm being unfaithful and cowardly and risking my life. But that's what happens when you lose hope and you need to fuck to distraction and every time I am inside him I think of *The Deer Hunter* and my cock goes so hard I shoot. You've read my stories, you know my work, I don't need to tell you that death is an aphrodisiac. Henry has the dick of death. I've heard his stories and I know: His rectum will be my grave.

How much longer do you need to stay away from me, sweetness? How much time do you need to be with those Americans in that isolated Emily Dickinson house? I can't find reasons to get up in the morning and you're floating across your porch in linen trousers and a tight white T-shirt. It's even harder when there's someone with me and I have to make morning talk. Can you tell someone you've slept with, someone who's a stranger to your inner world, can you tell them you can't imagine any reason to get out of bed? Can you say that to a stranger? With you I could. We'd been together a week, or maybe in the first few minutes into our relationship, and I said: Sweetness, I hate my life. I hate the thought of a continual present. And you held me, remember, in your arms on that massive Habitat sofa of yours with Fauré's *Requiem* playing in the background. And you said: I'm here, my love.

I'm writing to tell you that I've given the sofa to the council. The living room looks better without it, more space to dance, and the refugees who got it need it more than we do. The sofa was not the first thing to go. All this clutter, the trinkets and ornaments and objets d'art you keep bringing back from around the world. I'm sorry, but I can't collude with such clutter. It's your imperialist British blood that makes you accumulate all that stuff from remote outposts. Oxfam has it all now. At first they were reluctant, because they don't usually pick stuff up, but when the couple came they were so nice. The Nigerian woman said she might even take a few pieces for herself. I invited them to stay for a while and made a pot of tea and we sat on the Persian rug in the living room and they said I was lucky to have someone like you. They did. The woman said she was always falling in love with psycho-dykes. The guy was a Quaker from Newcastle, with long blonde dreads, doing an MA in Development Studies at SOAS. He smiled a lot. They do that, Quakers: Smiling and keeping silent in circles. After they left, I cried for about three hours and then I called the Gay and Lesbian Switchboard because by then there was only a silk curtain between me and the craft knife.

The Switchboard thought I was entertaining and intelligent. They thought I was so full of hope they didn't see how they could help. I think the guy, Andrew, wanted to meet up. I mean, he knows what I look like and he's read my book and seen all the stories I've published. I said: You can write me a letter if you like. Send it to my publisher and they'll forward it to me. He said: I will. I will. Thank you. I think you're wonderful. I'm, I mean, me and my friends are big fans. So to stop myself from crying after I put the phone down I began to drink and once I was drunk I called Henry, and said: Henry, sweetness, come be with me.

Henry brought tulips and slices of carrot cake. Henry took me to bed and held me. I told him I preferred cuddling in bed to that old over-priced Habitat sofa. I've always hated that sofa. He said: Fucking hell, where's the Habitat sofa, I've never sat on nothing from Habitat. The bed is an island in the corner of the room and we lie under the duvets and Henry tells me more stories. He tells me the one about his father. Are you sure you want to hear this? When he was twelve his father said to him: Don't kiss me anymore. And this, too: Henry has a very large dick and when I sucked on it, or rather, when I tried to get most of it into my mouth he said: I got that from my dad. And I said: Did he have a big penis, too? And Henry said: Yeah, I saw it, I saw it when it was hard. And all the while he's telling me this I'm slurping on his cock and thinking: There's stuff you're trying to tell me, Henry, and I'm not sure I want to know. After he came in my mouth, he said: Now tell me about *your* dad.

Henry knows everything. You know the story so I'm not going to repeat it. I don't expect you to hear this story more than once. After I told it to Henry he said: Fucking hell, what a bastard. Where is he, the bastard? And then I rolled on top of him and kissed him, especially on his eyelids, and he said: You can fuck me now. I put my lips against his and whispered into his mouth: What did you say? So Henry said it again.

Can you see how I latch onto other people's stories? It's the only way I'll be able to rescue myself if you don't come home? I'll engage with as many types as possible, bring home the guy who sells the *Big Issue* outside Woolies, the guy who plays the didjeridoo in Covent Garden, old men from the Duke of Wellington, cruise the cemetery until I find someone with a story to tell. Are you listening? Are you hearing what I'm saying? Can you see I'm just one step away from madness, nothing left to hold onto. It's imperative you return to our abode. Promptly. Toot sweet, sweetness. Are you following me, are you with me, are you sitting down, pouring another drink? First the gin then the ice then the tonic then the lime. Are you putting the letter down after every few pages and going inside for another drink? What do you drink there: Southern Comfort? Rye? Bourbon? Martinis? Isn't that what they drink in big houses in Maine with tongueless women running around gulping martinis with stuffed olives swallowed whole? Do you have guests? Do they ask about me? Do you say: Actually, I've just received another letter from him. God, I miss that man.

It's okay to come home now, sweetness. I told Henry to go and I told the other men never to contact me. I said: My boyfriend's coming home, I need to get the house ready. I'm dusting everything and hoovering and I'm doing lots of cooking, freezing, for when he gets back so we can spend the first few days getting reacquainted and we won't have to worry about preparing food. We can pop a lasagne in the oven. I'll make moussaka and humous and rice. Your favourite rice with cumin and almonds and raisins. We'll eat in bed and you can tell me about the Americans and what they said to you, show me pictures of the house, the lake, that porch. I want to know everything, because you've been so good to me, listening to everything, insisting on the details.

I'm writing to tell you I'm sorry. There. I said it. I'm sorry. I am. This is not a ploy. This is a genuine watchamacallit. I love you. God, don't you know that? Can I tell you what it's like without you? It's raw flesh, no skin, just exposed meat. I walk around and people are sandpaper against me, making me bleed, especially people I know whom I meet in the street and they want to know how I am, then wait to be asked similar questions. There's something you need to know: I've changed since you left. I am not the same person.

I'm writing to tell you that the man (not Henry) arrived, unannounced, and said he had no plans to move. So I made him bangers and mash and fried onions with gravy and we tried, or at least I tried to make meaningful conversation. I thought, well, maybe when you get back, sweetness, we could all go out together. He told me about a painting he's working on, a landscape from memory. He said it was a painting painted in a trance. I said: Isn't it strange when you meet new people and discover you have things in common, similar likes and dislikes, but when you come to mention them you feel like a silly copy-cat with no will or life of your own. I said: That's how I write sometimes. And he said: Is that a fact? He said: My painting takes up the whole wall in my warehouse. You see, he wants to be able to move while painting and when he finally exhibits the painting he'll put it in a narrow room so people will have to walk along the picture with no way of keeping their distance.

I'm writing to tell you that the man is still in our bed. He's a night person and he sleeps most of the morning, so I'm in the garden, laptop and all, writing to you. The sun is out and the clouds are pure cotton wool (a cliché, I know, but aren't all clichés based in reality, like: I love you. Like: You take my breath away). Listen to the sycamore tree in the wind behind me. Listen to the clouds moving across the sky.

I'm writing to let you know what we did last night and into the early hours of the morning. You said you wanted to know everything, so I'm going to tell you that he's one of the better kissers I've known and that his mouth is receptive and sometimes when I'm above him, his cock inside me, he arches his back, lifts his head up and opens his mouth, tongue out like a gosling, and I want to cry. His nipples are hard so I can nibble on them as much as I like, until I become overwhelmed by his pleasure and bite them off.

I'm writing to tell you that I'm not sure whether to wake Henry. Do you want me to tell him to go? I will if you want me to. If you're going to be here by the end of the week I'll tell him to go. He needs to get up and leave anyway. Last night he told me he had to get some paints, check the *a-n* for exhibitions to submit to, see his agent, buy cat food, apply for a two-month residency in a remote Irish castle. Something like your mansion in Maine, I suspect, but without the women who carry their tongues around in purses. Do you think all artists are like you and that he'll run away in the end?

I'm writing to tell you that Henry's not been in our bed for a while and that I called the other men to make sure they know never to come back. I told them my boyfriend's coming home. I said: I'm buying a new bed, getting rid of the old one, you must never come to this house again. Then I called the council's big items removal service. They've been so nice to me. I got to speak to the same woman I spoke to last time and she said she'd send someone to collect the old bed. I said it was in excellent condition, that we've always covered the mattress with protective sheeting. That's good, sir, she said, when's a convenient time to come round?

I'm writing to tell you that the coast is clear. By the time you get back there'll be a new bed and if you like we can go shopping for a sofa. Nothing too flash, maybe a second-hand sofa from Cookson's off Church Street, something that comes with its personality intact. I'll send this letter off and expect to hear from you in a few days. I'll have it all sorted by then. The house will be clean, the garden will be tidy, and the daffodils will be blooming. Everything will be fresh and spotless and completely new.

Myths of this Place

I went to New York to visit my brother who'd been living there for a couple of years, and although I was in my mid-thirties I'd never been to America. I'd read the books and seen the movies – I felt as if I knew New York – so when I got off the plane (I'd flown in from my cousin's wedding in LA) it was like walking into my own fantasy of the city. I'd wanted to hail a bright yellow cab and tell the guy, "Hey, buddy, there's a hundred bucks in it for you if you get me to Brooklyn by noon. Step on it, pal." I did say something to that effect, but it definitely wasn't a hundred, and we drove into Brooklyn, me in the back of the cab feeling lightheaded and exhilarated, windows open, hot air blowing into my face like I was back in the desert we grew up in.

There'd been a moment while driving into the city, when I thought: This sure ain't London. Fuck London. Give me New York City any day. I didn't care that it was scorching hot and my back was sticking to my shirt, the whole of me plastered to the taxi's leather seat. I wanted to get to my brother's apartment and take the Subway into Manhattan and walk through the Village, those streets that have been part of my psyche for years, since long before I ever thought I'd get here – the myths of this place, poems and stories that have steered me through the years. It had always been enough to know that New York existed, a kind of promised land, more than San Francisco, more than London. I tell myself that England is more suited to my disposition, though, the melancholy, the gloom, my tendency to deny myself the pleasures of the body, though this will soon change in New York, with me in Central Park at midnight.

I met Hilton downstairs at Monster Bar, opposite The Stonewall Inn. Later, we walked to Central Park and found a bench in a secluded spot and he sat down and unzipped his trousers and took out his cock and I'd knelt before him, just like that. He was recently back from Afghanistan, or maybe Iraq, and all that evening he'd talked about the pain in his tooth, a throbbing ache at the back of his mouth, a wisdom tooth rotting that was about to be extracted the next day.

He liked to call me baby.

"It's just me and you, baby," he said when this old man stood behind us and exposed himself.

I'd never been called baby before, not by anyone, and I wanted to flee and I wanted to crumble. It was that kind of time in my life, probably one of the worst. But New York was glorious. It was hot, even at night, and Hilton and I were invincible. In pain, but invincible.

"Keep sucking my pee-pee," he said.

"Your pee-pee?" I said, smiling up at him.

"Yes," he said, his hand on the back of my head.

I wasn't ready for an audience. That would come a few years later.

We went to a bar on 74th Street, down a couple of stairs from the sidewalk. I ordered a beer and Hilton drank rum and Coke and we sat at the bar like regulars. A small rock behind the counter had the words FAIRIES WELCOME chiseled into it, and Hilton knew the bartender, which, too, made me happy, like I belonged, like I was making connections, because after three years of scraping around in London and keeping the wolves from the door and various other clichés of the clichéd writer's struggle, I'd come to realize that London was not a good place to be alone and penniless. Nobody poor was doing anything interesting, not the kind of writing and art that had kept me going for so many years. Like the writers of New York who'd been scribbling and sweating for the past forty years in Andrew Holleran's *Dancer*, in Melvin Dixon's *Changing Rooms*, David Wojnarowicz's diaries, Jane DeLynn's *Don Juan* and all the stories of love and sex and the Everard Baths and the Anvil, everything that had been handed down to me, the topography of my soul, transmitted through my DNA as if this is what my real ancestors had been doing since long before I was born, and suddenly I'm here to find out where I'm from – this is where I'm from! – my roots are in New York, the dew of its grass still wet on my knees.

At my cousin's wedding in LA, I'd oscillated between feeling untouchable and imagining myself as a hipster, especially that night at Bar Marmont, beneath the hotel where John Belushi died, my cousin and I watching the maitre d' from our table, thick eye-shadow, rouge on his cheeks, false eyelashes, tight snake-skin trousers, and his bright blue shirt open to reveal a chest all pumped and freshly waxed. We ate oysters and shrimp tamales, dim sum, tuna steak, salmon in pastry with horseradish and salsa. We drank cosmopolitans and smoked – was it that long ago? – and at some point a young man, Mick, a boy of about twenty came up to ask for a cigarette, and stood with us, his arm brushing mine. I remember staring at him, fascinated by the vast expanse of his American youth, its energy, which gradually sapped some of my own.

"So," he said. "You guys live here, or you just visiting the fine city of LA?"

"He's from London," my cousin said.

"London?" the guy said. "Now, London is cool. London is cooler than this place."

Just the thought of home made me despair, that moment I'd have to walk through the door, manoeuvre my suitcase past the upstairs neighbour's bicycle, lodged there in the entrance hall, everything small and dingy, a dirty place to come back to: the stained carpet, the grimy wallpaper. I couldn't bear to be in that house. I'd stretched my misery to its limit. I've always lived like that, waiting for the point of no return, not trusting my desire until it was almost too late. For a long time I lived the almost-too-late life.

"You want another drink, baby?"

"Sure," I said.

"Kiss me, baby."

"Sure," I said.

I was grateful then for those shadowy places, caverns to escape to after dark, engulfing, so that when we came back out onto the street the brightness of the city was a surprise, especially so late at night. We walked toward the subway station, me catching glimpses of myself in shop windows, as if a ghost was following us down Broadway, not Hilton, myself but not myself, me as unrecognizable. The ghost looked like my father, who by then had been dead for six months, but there I was, having crossed an ocean and a continent, encountering the ghost of a man with hair darker than mine, almost as tall as me. I didn't say anything, not to Hilton, who was still focused on the sharp pain in his jaw, his rotting tooth.

We stood together at the entrance to the subway, him about to get on a train to the Bronx, me in the other direction, eventually to change to the F that would get me to Brooklyn. He was beautiful, perfectly formed in that American way, every part of his flesh the right proportion, a body built for battle or porn, which sometimes amounts to the same thing. We were kissing by then, aware that what others would be seeing was a white man and a black man embracing, and I thought about *Another Country* and Wallace Thurman. Then it started to rain, a slight drizzle, an attempt at a respite from the heat, tiny drops catching the light from the street-lamps so that it seemed like the air was streaked with glitter and I said, "See you tomorrow." And he said, "Yes, baby, yes, see you tomorrow."

There'd been a eureka moment flying in from LA, somewhere over the Rockies, me by the window eating Oreo cookies, and I'd decided, I will enjoy New York and everything it has to offer, I will make the most of my time there. Misery and discomfort had become my addiction, and like my father, or perhaps because of my father, I did not trust joy. At the wedding, my uncle had told me a story about sitting with my dad on the beach in Malibu some years back. They'd just been deep-sea fishing, and now they were back home after hiking in the hills, and my father had said to my uncle, "There's something wrong with this country. Nothing can be so good." My uncle reassured him: Things really were that good.

I can tell you one thing that is wrong with New York: The waiters! They rush you, become proprietary, mark their territory, make it clear they will be taken into account. You cannot ignore them. In New York, there is always the waiter to include in the equation. He is a witness, a servile lover, a bossy bottom. Those were the kinds of thoughts I'd been having that afternoon at Franelli's on Prince Street, pretty much straight from the airport, while my brother was at work, before I'd met Hilton and we'd landed up in Central Park around midnight... or perhaps the whole waiter thing happened later during the visit, but I definitely went to Franelli's, because that was the afternoon they played Van Morrison, and hearing his voice took me back to my father's hospital bed and my mother saying to me, "He was a best friend. We had fun. We did things together. We liked reading the same books, listening to the same music. But Van Morrison," my mother said, "I could never understand how he liked him."

And since then, Van Morrison keeps appearing in unexpected places, like the week before New York in the shop at the Getty, Van Morrison murmuring through the speakers, a whisper from my dad. I kept quiet about it, didn't say anything to my cousin. I've learned that sometimes sharing a memory can dilute it.

By mid-morning, temperatures had past 35 degrees Celsius – 95 degrees Fahrenheit, the TV news said – and I was feeling trapped in my brother's apartment, housebound by the heat as if there was nowhere to escape to, not even to the coolness of Starbucks on 7th Avenue. I had to get out, to move, to create my own breeze. Walking toward Prospect Park, the city's intense heat creating its own music, television noises from open windows, the whirr of air conditioning units, the way some buildings seemed to crack like parched earth. No one sweated as much as I did. It was as if I couldn't keep my pores closed, as if I were opening up, leaking out, as if my entire insides were melting, everything would come rushing out at any moment. My Chinese doctor back in London had said I was the kind of person who couldn't hold onto good things, that I arrive empty, purge myself before I go in, create a vacuum that gets filled with dread and shame and self-doubt.

I considered going into the cinema on Prospect Park West, but *Frequency*, *Gladiator* and *Keeping the Faith* were not movies I wanted to see, so I took the train to Coney Island, expecting to find, as they'd promised in the in-flight magazine, decayed grandeur. What I found were people selling used car parts, faded CDs, clothing from the 60s, furry toys, everything bleached by too-long in the sun. The game arcades were open but empty, loud music blared from their doorways, vast counters of hot dog vendors were selling cheese dogs and onion rings, French fries, cheese fries. I'd stood in the queue for hot dogs at Nathan's Famous, transfixed by the woman behind the counter, her accent twangy. I lost my patience and headed towards the beach, past boarded-up restaurants and hot dog stands, Mama's Italian Ices, the fun-fair rides, many of them brown from rust. Two Hasidic boys got into cars on the racing track. The guy on duty kept announcing over his megaphone, "Your gas is on the right, breaks on the left," over and over until I was too far away to hear, the sound of the waves on the shore drowning out all other noises.

I bought some corn and onion rings from the Grill Bar on the boardwalk and sat on a bench by the sea. A couple was playing in the shallow water, others were in sleeping bags on the sand. The air was cooler. I could feel it on my feet, in the new sandals I'd bought from a wholesale place near my brother's flat. "Crunchy granola lesbian sandals," he'd called them, and then he'd gone off to a class (he was an actor), then to work, so I only saw him late at night, sometimes in the mornings. Since our father's death we seemed to appreciate each other's company more, as if he and I were fragments, ricochets, reminders of what we loved about him.

Later, in Washington Square, waiting for Hilton, I'd watched three young men playing hacky sack and a guy with a guitar singing "No Woman, No Cry." Paused in my lostness, my frantic wandering through streets, there, surrounded by people, something bigger than me, and, like the sea, it calmed me, allowed me to disappear for a while. I kept my eyes on the singer, tall and slim, until he spotted me and smiled, quickly and easily, which is when Hilton turned up and sat down, nudged me, looked across to where I was looking and smiled at the guy and shrugged in a way that said, He's mine, and the guy smiled back.

"How did it go?" I said.

"It went," he said, and took his tooth from his pocket, neatly wrapped in gauze. "For the tooth fairy," he said. "Extra cash for my birthday."

"When is it?" I said.

"Friday," he said.

"I'll be gone by then," I said.

Then he produced two tickets from his back pocket. "We'll celebrate tonight." he said.

A friend of his had to go on a work trip and had offered Hilton the tickets: seats to the opening night of Keith Jarrett at Carnegie Hall.

"But I thought he was sick," I said, the tender notes

of the Köln Concert already playing in my head.

"Not any more."

May has always been the month of birthdays, especially when I was growing up, a couple of friends at school, my father, my nanny, my cousin in LA, then Simon and Viktor, both of them lovers, one killed by the virus, the other, for all I know, still with his wife. May has brought many men I have loved into the world.

When we got to Carnegie Hall, our seats were so high up that Hilton went to one of the ushers and said his boyfriend – his boyfriend! – suffered from vertigo and could we sit somewhere else. The guy led us to better seats. "Thank you, gay mafia," Hilton whispered as we descended two flights and were offered the latecomer seats on the side, padded stand-alone chairs where we sat and waited for Keith Jarrett.

As if he'd returned from the dead. Illness had silenced him, kept him in the underworld, but now he was back, walking onto the stage. The audience rose to its feet, waited for him to reach his piano, just him and the piano on stage, and he sat down, and we sat down, and his long fingers tapped the keys, touching but not touching, the first gentle notes of "It's All in the Game," the words to which I knew from an old Van Morrison cover. I mouthed them as he played, a song that began with many a tear has to fall and I kept going, my hand in the hand of the man next to me, smiling at each other, following the lyrics in silence till the final words that promised that our hearts would fly away.

But that's not how it happened, not the last scene, not the ending.

What really happened was that my mother bought my brother and I tickets to see Keith Jarrett. She wouldn't be travelling anywhere for the next few months, not till the year of mourning was over, so she wanted us to go for her. Dad would have wanted you to be there. So we sat in those seats reserved for latecomers, my brother and I, and we smiled and looked at each other as Keith Jarrett began to play and we knew we were thinking similar thoughts, perhaps about my father's joy in the face of such beauty, his love of rhythm that we'd inherited, how he'd taken us out of South Africa all those years ago and driven us across Europe in a VW camper van, music blaring from the speakers – Stevie Wonder, Earth, Wind and Fire, the soundtrack to our exodus. And now, after almost twenty years in the desert, we are dispersed again, each of us on a continent of his own, bound together by a man who is no longer with us, but keeps reappearing in mysterious ways.

Leaving Tel Aviv

The hairdresser on Ben Yehuda Street tells me her uncle smuggled her out of Morocco when she was five and brought her to Israel. He helped others escape until he was caught, interrogated, sent to prison for a couple of years, then eventually made his way to Israel with her parents, and the family was reunited. She's in her mid-fifties, hair dyed blonde, fingers nimble with scissors and comb. It's a Friday afternoon, that liminal time of the week in most parts of Israel. It's my last weekend here. On Monday I'll be back in London.

"Do you like it there?" she says.

After twenty years, I tell her, I'm about ready to leave. My life is divided into chunks: first South Africa, then Israel, now London. I tell her that for the last five years I've been waiting for the right moment, the catalyst to facilitate my exit. Barcelona is one of the options. In Tel Aviv it had been the same: for my last few years living there, I dreamt of escape. I'm good at beginnings, the drama of wooing and seduction, the honeymoon phase. That's what it's like with me and relationships, I'm not very evolved when it comes to attachment.

Earlier that day (although I don't tell her this) I'd been to the Muslim cemetery near the hotels on the beachfront. A derelict place with sun-bleached tombs like blocks of concrete amongst dusty shrubs. A white cat roams the parched earth like a ghost. I'd planned to take pictures, maybe write something. Not many people in Tel Aviv know there's a cemetery there, right in the middle of the city, behind a stone wall that flanks the path that runs along the cliff. A guy with a large DV camera on his shoulder is filming the place. We get talking. He's from the Waqf, the Muslim charity that oversees the upkeep of sacred sites.

"We need to do something about this," he says.

He takes me to the spot where people have been having sex on mouldy mattresses, amongst discarded condoms.

"The ho... ho..." he says, struggling with a word I assume will be homeless, but turns out to be homos. I don't tell him that these are my people, that I, too, used to pick up men not far from here in Independence Park. "The hotel," he says, pointing, "stands on the other half of the cemetery."

That's the kind of place Tel Aviv is. If you take in what's around you, the onslaught of history will drive you crazy. Everyone's in some stage of recovery from trauma. The Naqba and the Holocaust are never far away. It's easy not to know this. The food is good and plentiful, cafés are open till late, the weather's glorious, people are beautiful, it doesn't take much effort to get laid.

When I think of my years in Tel Aviv, I think mainly of the two years on Sheinkin Street, in that flat with its large balcony overlooking a backyard cluttered with broken furniture. I lived there with Melissa first, then Pierre. Those years were my last years in the military. When I finished the army I came to London for a while, but homesickness got the better of me, and I went back to what I knew. Even though I eventually did get away and have been in London all this time, Tel Aviv is still, although I don't often admit to this, one of my heart-homes.

Friday afternoons in Tel Aviv and the city changes pace. Everything becomes quieter during those winding-down hours: traffic thins out, people retreat into their homes in a siesta kind of way. When I lived on Sheinkin Street, on Friday mornings we'd clean the flat then go shopping for food, stocking up with fruit and vegetables from Carmel Market, a long street of fresh food stands, stalls with fake CK underwear, cheap T-shirts. The smell of fresh herbs and over-ripe fruit was everywhere. Around the corner from the market, there was a place that sold cheap alcohol, and where Pierre and I stocked up for the party we had during that summer we shared the flat on Sheinkin Street.

We knew people, but we didn't know many, so we walked around with invitations we'd had printed on business cards and handed them to cute guys on the street. People came. You could hardly move in the flat that night. At some point it got so loud, so crowded that I gave up changing the records and got increasingly drunk. In those days, I drank more than I smoked, although hash was always easy to come by. This guy I knew from the army grew it on his farm. Eventually the flat emptied out and a group of us went to the beach for a late swim, down through the market which was empty late at night, and being barefoot, like I often was, the rotting fruit squished between my toes.

Towards the bottom of Sheinkin Street, just before the market, there used to be a second-hand bookshop, Bibliophile, run by Albert, an old Algerian guy. He was short, a chain-smoker, as intense as a French intellectual. For the last two months of my army service, I worked in that shop. It was my first writerly job, although I'd already done some of the jobs writers do to include in their bios: bartender in a shitty bar where the shitty owner liked to fuck me, then sandwich maker at Señor Sandwich, one of the few places in the city where you could get ham, though we had to peel it off the sandwiches at the end of our shift to be used the next day. The rest of the leftovers we took home.

When I worked in the bookshop, I was having sex with a guy called Moshe, who'd been in an elite combat unit during the war in Lebanon. I remember how he used to shake when we were in bed, how he wanted me to hold him, his tight muscled body, and he'd tell me how he was in love with this guy from his unit, a guy from Jerusalem called Adam. They'd gone through the war together, the worst part of it: at one point they got stuck in a bombed-out building and huddled there in a corner clinging to each other, too afraid to do anything.

Cities are for sex. And the most licentious of them all are those cities by the sea. Even though Tel Aviv is hot and humid most of the year and there's not much room to breath with the buildings so close together, after a while you become addicted to the stuffiness, the decay, and you stop thinking about space. My people are used to ghettoes, familiar with confinement. Wide boulevards and sprawling parks are for the goyim. Nights can be as hot and sticky as the days, but it's when the city begins to exhale. The temperature drops slightly after the relentless and unforgiving sun has set, and like most Mediterranean ports, the city comes alive as a place of pleasure: eating and dancing and fucking.

And then there's the *mirpeset*.

Often in the summer we'd sleep on the balcony, or

make out in full view of the neighbours. Post-coital, we'd eat watermelon with salty Bulgarian cheese, read a book, or lie on the tattered sofa, desperate for a cool breeze. The *mirpeset* was the closest you got to a back garden. Balconies are in other cities, meant for other things, more genteel. Even when we speak English we use the Hebrew word. My new place has a great *mirpeset*. I love your *mirpeset*. People are sealing up their balconies now, extending the size of their living rooms. It's a bourgeois thing, but it's also a way of putting up walls. I grew up in South Africa. I've seen this happen.

Towards the end of my haircut, a guy comes into the salon. He's the hair products salesman, but he's not here to sell anything. He's in the neighbourhood, he says, though it feels like something's happening between him and the hairdresser. It's Friday, so we talk about *hamin*, that overnight, slow-cooked casserole of beans and potatoes and meat that Jews have been making for centuries. It goes by different names in different places: *Tbit* in Iraq, *cholent* in Europe. They compare recipes. His family's from Tehran and he's proud to be in charge of the *hamin* in his house.

By then my haircut's done and I leave them chatting, making a note-to-self to buy a *hamin* cookbook before flying back to London. I walk up along Ben Yehuda Street, take a left on Bugrashov, then head towards

Dizengoff Cente, Tel Aviv's first shopping mall. I love these side streets, the grimy pavements, the large ficus trees, the way people amble, the way in some cities it can feel like nobody ever goes to work. Cafés on every corner, chairs and tables outside, glass doors open to the street.

Tel Aviv is easy to love. It's crammed, crumbling and suffocating. Like other big cities – San Francisco, New York, Melbourne – it likes to think it's better than the rest of the country. London tends to do that, too: and in many ways it is, but at the end of the day you can't ignore what's going on around you.

I fell out of love with Tel Aviv, though it was more a falling out with the country, its politics, by which I mean its people. It became hard to love. After a few years of mild political activism, I stopped believing peace was possible. I saw the entrenchment of the occupation, the deepening of the Jewish right, the way their sentiments trickled down and poisoned the Left, the dehumanising of everything, the self, the other. No matter how much Tel Aviv pretends to be an entity unto itself, at some point you can't block out what's around you. For a long time, and probably still, I loved Tel Aviv for its smell and its heat and its people and its markets and its clubs and its beaches and its parks and also because of its trauma, the never-ending dramas that are the lives of the people who live there.

How do I tell the whole story of my Tel Aviv love affair? What do I pick that will, as Mary Oliver says, "cast its shadow or its light over the whole body of my telling"? Do I keep talking about the Sheinkin Street years and how, most Saturdays, we'd hitch-hike to the nudist beach just north of the city, how towards the end of those years my friend Sara got married to this cute Yemenite guy just so she could get out of the army. I was the designated wedding photographer, but somehow the film got lost on the way to be developed, so I hardly have any pictures of that time.

Or do I write about the Gulf War months in the early 1990s and the bombing of Tel Aviv, and how we sealed a room in the flat with tape on the windows, plastic sheeting over the doors, and hid behind the sofa, gas masks on, SCUD missiles being lobbed at us from Iraq. This was after we came back, after we'd initially run for safety to places like Eilat and Jerusalem, but in the end returned to Tel Aviv, bombs or no bombs. We wanted to be here. At night, before the sirens began we'd go out drinking and wheel each other through the streets in abandoned shopping trolleys, singing.

Most of the shops in Dizengoff Centre are closing for the Sabbath. In the inner courtyard downstairs, near the entrance to the cinema, a DJ is playing music for a crowd with headphones on. They dance to music only they can hear, so it looks like a kind of performance that has been going on all afternoon, but by now there are only ten or twelve people left on the dance floor. A fat girl is sweating profusely, the shadow of her spine imprinted on the back of her T-shirt. A young Japanese guy stands to one side, watching the last of the Sabbath revellers, his headphones cupping his ears, nodding gently in time to the music like one who, with serene conviction, is saying yes, yes, yes.

Some Hasidic Tales

This happened in 1980, a couple of years after we left South Africa and moved to Israel. Some friends were visiting from Port Elizabeth and I went to meet them in Jerusalem. We'ere walking on the outskirts of the Old City, along a wall that must have been the bastion of some Roman fortress, and this group of Orthodox men are below us – I don't remember how many, maybe just two – and from our elevated position on the wall, I spat at them. Maybe it was just a symbolic spitting, the kind that is more the sound of spitting, the kind we do three times to ward off the evil eye, or maybe I collected saliva from my cheeks to catapult at them.

I remember the look on my friend's face, one friend in particular, her embarrassment, like she'd just witnessed something she wished she hadn't. I told her, as if showing off my new fluency in the language, that people here hated the Orthodox. I don't remember if the men responded by looking up or walking faster, or if we sped up to get away from them. There was no hatred in my actions, at least not towards those men. I was aping the attitudes of my classmates, trying to fit in.

The second incident happened six or seven years later. I'd done my three years in the army and before starting my studies at Tel Aviv University, I moved into a flat on Shenkin Street. The neighbourhood has a large Orthodox community, several shuls, some yeshivas, the kids in the playground spoke Yiddish. Yet, not once in the five years I lived there, did I exchange a single word with any of them. During that time, I volunteered for The White Line, Israel's lesbian and gay switchboard. We'd get calls from yeshiva *bochers*, young men calling from a public phone, unsure what to do with their attraction to a boy in their class, or a young Orthodox guy would tell us he'd taken the bus into Tel Aviv and wanted to meet other men but didn't know how. God has never been part of my belief system, so the torment of his possible disapproval is unimaginable to me. I'd survived the closet, that penal colony of one, and grown up in a family, so I knew something of the threat of excommunication.

The summer before my courses started, I worked in the kitchen of a bar called Skizza. I was the cook and Dalia washed dishes. She was fifteen. She'd run away from her home in Bnei Brak, the Orthodox neighbourhood outside Tel Aviv, and lived in a backpackers hostel on Ha'Yarkon Street. I remember her telling me that she'd bumped into her father once near the Shalom Towers, and he'd told her never to come home, called her a whore. At the end of our shift at 4am, Dalia sitting side-saddle on the frame of my bicycle, my arms on either side of her, gripping the handlebars, I'd give her a lift back to the hostel. We laughed as we rode together along empty streets, the dawn sky turning purple, frantic birdsong in the trees along Allenby and Ben-Yehuda Streets, the air moist with dew and humidity.

I took any job I could get back then and worked for the guy who'd trained us as switchboard volunteers. He must have been in his late fifties. I think he made movies, so was well-known in the city. I figured if I took the job I'd make new friends. I was his cleaner. There was nothing sexy about it, not in cleaning for someone much older than me, not in the way he'd sit on the sofa and talk to me while I washed his floors. One weekend he invited me to a party. The one thing I remember from that party is that in the bedroom opposite the front door, two elderly Orthodox men in black, *payes* and long beards, were reclining on a double bed, the way you might with a lover you've been with for a long time, watching television at the end of the day. They never left the room to join the party. Apparently, they were rabbis, the heads of two yeshivas in Jerusalem. They liked being around other gay men, even though they never had sex. I remember feeling disappointed not to have met them.

There's another story that has come to me while writing this. An Orthodox family lived in a house outside the grounds of my high school in Ashkelon. The father was a rabbi. The daughter had learning difficulties and would stand at the fence and ask us to have sex with her, until her mother appeared at the kitchen door to call her back inside.

These stories feel like apparitions, images seen in a flash, from a distance.

The closest I got to spending time with Orthodox men was soon after I moved to London. One of my first jobs was teaching English to a group of *hasids* in Stamford Hill. The men were eager to learn, they wanted to be fluent, write in cursive, and know the grammar rules of English by the time term was up. If I'd known how to, if I'd had enough resources and experience to give them what they wanted, they would have retained everything. They were impatient, bursting with questions, curious, as if language itself were a spiritual undertaking. They didn't care about mundane stuff. I remember teaching them ordinal numbers – first, second, third – and drawing a picture of an Olympic podium on the board. None of them knew what I was talking about, and when I explained the sketch to them, they weren't particularly intrigued. They had no interest in the Olympic Games.

I loved their vitality, that moment when they'd step

into the room, take off their jackets, roll up their sleeves, their bodies supple, no longer stooped, hurrying, as if to avoid snipers. I enjoyed flirting with them, trying to shock them with my tattoos and piercings, which they cared about as much as they did the Olympics. I wanted to be in their group, to have the certainty they had, their hunger. I didn't last long in the job. Whatever reasons I gave at the time, the real reason was that I couldn't keep up, couldn't impart the knowledge at the rate they wanted. As much as I loved being able to give them something, and their willingness to accept, I wanted to be a part of them, not the odd one out.

That brief experience made me more comfortable being close to Orthodox Jews. Those four hours a week I spent in the classroom, the proximity of their bodies changed something in me. I liked being amongst them in North East London. They are my people, part of my messy and atavistic subconscious. We are all Jews in the Diaspora. During Hanukah I liked buying donuts from their bakeries, chopped herring from their fisheries, farfel from their grocery stores. I notice I'm saying "their" as if they are separate from my usual set of people, my ham-and-cheese-eating crowd.

A few week ago, just before the *seder* – I was in charge of the gefilte fish – I cycled up to Moishe's Supermarket on Dunsmure Road to buy matzo meal and horseradish sauce. The *seder* was the following day and the shop was full of men buying last-minute ingredients. Black coats everywhere, and a faint odour of unperfumed bodies. They chatted amongst themselves, talking on their mobile phones, urging their kids to decide which sweets they wanted. I stood in the queue and smiled, probably not just to myself, because a little boy, all golden-haired and wavy blonde *payes*, looked up at me with a frown on his face. I smiled at him, and he, as if he'd done this before and it was no big deal, extended his chin towards me and spat. No more than a few raindrops of spittle, but the sound was clear. It was the noise you make when your tongue shoots out between your lips. The father put his hand on the boy's shoulder and pulled him towards him, apologising.

"*Chag sameach*," I said.

"*Chag sameach*," he said, a split-second of surprise.

I want to say something about spitting, how it is both prophylaxis against bad luck and a gesture of contempt. Israelis spit on the Orthodox – metaphorically, or as I did, literally. Secular Jews will do anything they can to exorcise the stereotypical Jew from their midst. We don't like to be visible, exposed, made public to be sniped at. Secular Jews are also angry that the *Haredim* have laid claim to authentic Judaism and the state has gone along with it. Secular Jews aren't always sure what kind of Jews they want to be. I'm talking mainly about the 1980s and early 90s when I lived there. Maybe things are different today. Maybe they're worse.

In recent pictures from Israel's invasion into Gaza, cameras lingered on soldiers in *tallitot* and *tefillin* praying before going into battle. This turning to God might be indicative of a general loss of direction in Israel, the proliferation of the religious right, a way of returning to who we think we were. I don't remember such images from twenty years ago, all I remember is a general dismay at what we were getting ourselves into, a feeling that came back like a trauma when Israel again thought the best defence was attack.

As much as it might like to be, Israel is not a Western country. It is part of the madness that is the Middle East, far from life in the Diaspora. We are all looking for comfort: me in the Orthodox neighbourhoods of London, those terrified soldiers in the faith of the Orthodox. We are all on some level nostalgic for the ghetto, a people defined by longing, not belonging. Being amongst the *Haredim* in my London neighbourhood is the closest I'll ever get to being back in Port Elizabeth, Pesach time at the Summerstrand Shul, my first and second cousins, my grandparents, aunts and uncles, most of my family gathered together at the same time, joking, gossiping, passing around my grandfather's tin of snuff, praying in words that still made no sense to any of us.

Frozen Years

Pierre met a guy called Clayton who'd came to Israel for I'm not sure what. Clayton was tall, from Boston, and he thought that Pierre, a short man with wispy hair, almost balding, was the sexiest thing he'd ever met. I remember when Clayton said this. We were in the kitchen in the flat Pierre and I shared in Tel Aviv, watching him dress the salad he'd just made.

"Just look at that," Clayton said. "Isn't that just the sexiest thing?"

It was a long summer, as summers always are in Israel, stretching from April to October, grabbing up most of the year, peaking in August. We spent our free days on the beach or in air-conditioned cafés and cinemas. The French filmswere our favourites that summer, the Alan Rohmer ones, like *Le Rayon Vert*, in which people met up on their *vacances* and talked and ate and made love. We had the *vacances* weather but we were definitely not on *vacances*. I was still in the army. Pierre worked in a restaurant. Most of the people we knew in those days where either soldiers or waiters.

Our two-roomed flat was on the first floor of a rundown building on Sheinkin Street, a typical Tel Aviv building, three storeys with large balconies that look out onto the street, or, like ours, onto a backyard with weeds and discarded furniture. We lived on the less fashionable end of Sheinkin, close to the post office on Yehuda Ha'Levi and to a secret military base. Our building had no entrance door, and in the lobby, plaster fell from the ceiling in chunks and slid into the blue mailboxes nailed to the wall. The mailboxes were covered in stickers with the names of people who'd moved out, flatmates who'd left, new ones who'd taken their place.

The building was so run down there were no *va'ad bayit* fees to pay, though once in a while the lawyer who looked after the building for her Argentinian client sent a young guy to wash the stairs and collect the rubbish – all those cans and chocolate wrappers passers-by threw onto the patch of ground at the front of the building as if it were a public trash heap.

Pierre and I never talked about the war. He'd been in the tanks, gone up to Beirut, but refused to enter the city. I'd been on a base near the Syrian border where we spent our days patrolling for roadside-bombs or sitting in bunkers staring at mounds of soil on the opposite hill. The Syrians, I imagine, stared back. At night, the silence was tense with an overwhelming fear that we'd be attacked. Pierre and I never spoke of any of this, none of us did, not about the massacre in the refugee camps, nor about the young man we'd captured near our base and tied up and kept on the floor in the office until the interrogators came to pick him up. Our officers lived in a villa on a hill overlooking the valley, a grand house whose owners lived in Marseilles and had given the army, so we were told, permission to occupy their home.

During the day there was the beach and the movies, but at night there was The Park. Two or three times a week I'd be there, sometimes straight from the base, and I'd sit on a bench facing the horizon, the sea stretched out before me, ears pricked for the sound of footsteps on gravel, a potential lover? It was that time of evening when people arrived home from work, the relief at the end of a day, the scorching sun setting, a cool breeze coming off the water. If it was still light, I'd watch the deck-chair attendant folding and piling his chairs, tying them together with a metal chain.

On a night like this, I met Pierre.

He was being pursued by an older man, so he sat down next to me, pretended we knew each other.

"How's it going?" he said.

"I know that guy," I said.

"Can we talk about something else?" he said.

We talked about art and music – we both wanted to be actors – but mainly we talked about the guys we'd had sex with, probably as a way of working out what kind of sex we were about to have. We laughed a lot. We were in our early twenties. We hardly said "no" to anything. That was twenty-five years ago. So when Pierre finally said: "Do you want to have sex?" I said: "Sure." And we took a cab back to my place.

The sex wasn't great, and I hardly remember what we did, but our friendship was uninhibited and effortless. Pierre was living with his parents at the time, so it made sense for him to move into the second bedroom. We lived well together for most of that time, until the day I did what I did.

Pierre had another man after Clayton. Another man from later that summer. A guy called Turo, a dancer from Colombia, who'd run away from Bogota and landed up in Tel Aviv working with the Bat Sheva Dance Company. Slim and dark, a mix of Indian and African, he was the man who stayed the longest. His love for Pierre was absolute and gentle, and Pierre would stare at him in wonder, as if he'd fallen, like some Marquesian angel, out of the sky and onto the sofa on our balcony.

Back in 1984, Israel was still at war. Lebanon was our Vietnam. We were soldiers and protestors, veterans and hippies. I fucked around a lot, met all sorts of people. We all seemed to be fucking around a lot. AIDS was happening elsewhere. We had other life-and-death issues to worry about.

I remember one Saturday night sitting with Pierre on the floor in the kitchen – the coolest place in the flat – eating cheese and pickle sandwiches and drinking Goldstar Beer. Something like Chopin's *Nocturnes* must have been playing on the turntable, the first side of the record almost finished, when there was a knock on the door. I got up to open. The driver who'd chatted me up on the #5 bus earlier that week, was standing there with his dog.

"Maybe it's not a good time," he said, looking over my shoulder towards the kitchen where Pierre had stuck his head out from the doorway, just a few centimetres off the ground.

"What a gorgeous dog!" Pierre said, waving, his French accent more pronounced than usual.

"I'll be back in a minute," I said.

I took the bus-driver up onto the roof. I knew what he wanted, he'd told me already. His wife was American, they'd been together for ten years. There was something desperate and hungry about him. I fucked him under the warm night sky, against the sink where we did our laundry on those weekends we couldn't afford the laundromat. I remember his beautiful grey dog standing by the sink catching drops of water on its tongue. I remember thinking that this is the most wonderful thing, to be able to go upstairs with no sense of guilt or worry, no fear at all, have sex with a man, then kiss him at the top of the stairs – it's the right thing to do after sex with a stranger – and then go back to the kitchen where a good friend is waiting to pick up where we left off.

I came across Pierre's profile recently on Facebook and thought a lot about why I wanted to send him a message. To apologise, to make things better, set things straight, make amends. If I'm honest, I wanted to recapture something of that time, that closeness we had, the ease of our intimacy, the heat of Tel Aviv, those tiled floors under bare feet, the lovers we gossiped about. I wanted all that – the humidity, the drama, everything – because there is a part of me that is afraid to admit that perhaps the last twenty years of living where I live now, in this cold Northern country, have been a mistake, a way of blanking out the sense of injustice, the corruption, the corrosion that bleeds into every aspect of life in Israel, that these years away from there have been years of unreality. Frozen years.

I contacted Pierre because I want to believe we could go back to where things started to go wrong and do it differently, be friends again. I thought about responses I might get, something surprisingly kind, light and almost joking, as if to say: Ah, we were kids then (because we were) or maybe something deservedly harsh, vindictive. I wanted to believe that we'd be able to talk about it and everything would be forgiven. I know it's naïve, but he was my link to that time, the only person who can take us back there. So I sent him a message.

"Is that you?" I said, and waited.

On Saturday mornings we used to get up early, put on our uniforms without berets or boots, just sandals or flip-flops, and walk to Derech Haifa – the road that leads north out of Tel Aviv – and hitch a ride up the coast. It was easy to get cars to stop if you were in uniform, especially if you looked like a combat soldier in those loose, faded trousers and maroon paratrooper boots, which we'd managed to get hold of somehow even though by then we all had clerical jobs on various bases around Tel Aviv.

I'd been in Lebanon the year before, the year before that summer, the summer I'm remembering, the summer we spent our Saturdays on the beach. During my time in Lebanon I never saw the sea, though for a few months our unit was based near Lake Karoun and we swam between patrols and guard duty, until snipers began taking pot-shots at us from the hills, and we had to start wearing helmets and bullet-proof jackets wherever we went.

Now I live in a Northern country far from Tel Aviv. The cold keeps me intact, whole, separate. The cold inhibits movement, makes you want to wrap up. It's different in the heat. Heat joins you to others, to things, to everything. It's impossible to be distinct when you're constantly sweating, melting into the world. That summer, in all the confusion of sweat and heat and lust and listening to Chopin, I did something that surprised me because it was a first, and like having sex for the first time, like being fucked for the first time, rimmed, sucked off, whatever, it was something to add to my repertoire of – what? I don't know. Things to do with other people? But from that summer onwards, I'd be able to say: I am the sort of person who betrays a friend. I was, as someone else said to me years later and under different circumstances, lacking in human kindness.

Turo, the Columbian dancer, and I almost had sex before we had sex – it happened a few weeks before Pierre came home with him from I don't remember where, probably The Park. Pierre was good at chatting guys up. Or maybe it was Turo who did the chatting up.

I met Turo on the street.

It was late at night, earlier that same summer. I'd been jogging by the beach and was making my way home, turning off Allenby Street and running along Rothschild Boulevard, when a man cycled up alongside me. We carried on like this down the boulevard – him cycling, me running, occasionally looking at each other, smiling – all the way until I turned onto Sheinkin Street and he kept going. The man on the bike had been Turo. The next time I'd see him was with Pierre.

What will we talk about if Pierre writes back? About the war? The parties we went to? Dancing at Divine till five in the morning? Those months of living together – what were we thinking? How did we land up fighting, and over what? Over a man who neither of us ever saw again.

One evening, Turo turned up at the flat barefoot, his T-shirt soaked in sweat, saying he'd forgotten where we lived. He'd gotten off the bus outside Ichilov Hospital and walked all the way to our place from Weizman Street.

"I knew it was in the south," he said. "But I couldn't remember where exactly."

He scratched his stomach as if ants were crawling beneath his skin.

"I asked people if they knew you," he said.

"Let's walk," I said.

Along Sheinkin Street and onto Rothschild Boulevard where people were walking their dogs, old couples sat on wooden benches facing the boulevard, so that what was happening – the walking of the dogs, the Filipina nannies with their kids, the yeshiva *bochers* on their way to and from prayers – were like some great drama, actors criss-crossing a stage.

"I have to lie down," Turo said. "I'm tired."

"Keep walking," I said.

But his feet gave way and he flopped down onto the gravel in the middle of the boulevard.

"Is he okay?" a woman called from her bench.

"Should I call an ambulance?" the man in the kiosk said.

I waved at them and smiled and shook my head and tried to get Turo to stand up.

"Let's get back to the flat," I said.

"It's hard to get up," he said.

"Arturo," I said. "What pills did you take?"

"Blue," he said, curling up with his knees close to his chest. "Or red. What colour is LSD? Isn't it white? Do they come in all the colours? Where did Amir get them? Let's warn him."

"You'll have to get up for that," I said.

"Okay," he said. "Let's go home. Maybe Pierre will be back by now."

"Pierre's with his parents," I said. "He won't be back until Sunday."

A week later, when I got home from the base, Pierre was in the kitchen, at that small narrow table in that small narrow kitchen holding a glass of water.

"Were you going to tell me?" he said.

"About what?" I said.

"Yes," he said. "About what?" and he stood up and threw the water at me.

I moved towards him, punched him on the arm, pushed him so that he fell towards the balcony door. I filled another glass and flung the water at him. We fought. We landed up on the bed in my room – I don't remember how – and tried to pin each other down. We were sweating and wet from the water. And then I spat at him. I didn't think and I didn't stop myself. I spat. It was a way of expelling him, of expelling my guilt and my disgust with myself. Then he spat back. We'd been friends for over a year, a long time since we'd fumbled around and called it sex, then laughed about it when we told people how once we thought we could be lovers. And I realised, as I pinned his arms to the bed like in some childish game of Surrender, that Pierre still wanted to have sex, and I wanted to hurt him for that. He was, as my mother would say, a hoverer, and in the world of my childhood, hovering was the ultimate crime. It meant indecision. It meant having an unspoken desire. It meant cowardice, submission. And worst of all, it meant: I need you.

"How could you do it?" Pierre said.

"I don't know," I said, because I didn't, because I don't think I knew why I did anything in those days.

When you write the word Pierre in Hebrew, it can be read – if you don't use the vowels and the dot that differentiates the פ from the פ – as "fair." As in: *That's not fair.* Israelis use that phrase a lot. *Zeh loh fer*, meaning: That's not fair.

Pierre got off the bed and I stayed there, eyes closed, too ashamed to do anything. I listened to him opening the front door. I assumed he was carrying his stuff downstairs to a taxi or that he'd called a friend to come and pick him up. I thought of apologising. But I didn't. Maybe I didn't feel sorry. Maybe I assumed Turo wanted me more than Pierre and that made it somehow okay.

"It's never too late," a friend said recently when I told her the story. We were talking about things we regretted, which was how I got to thinking about Pierre.

The last thing I remember was the sound of the front-door key as he put it on the chest in the passageway between his bedroom and mine. I listened to him walking to the door. I hoped he'd turn the other way, towards the kitchen, then stop and peer into my bedroom and we'd say something to each other, anything.

Before things went wrong, we went to see a production of Verdi's *Falstaff*. Turo might have gotten us tickets through the ballet company, or maybe an ex of his was in it, something like that. As soon as the opera began, I thought: This is what we look like so much of the time, men together in a room, laughing. We must have looked like that – Pierre, Turo, me, and this young guitarist called Tom whom we'd met at a party – the four of us on the beach at five in the morning after dancing all night at Divine on Dizengoff Street. We left our clothes on the sand and swam out towards the wave breakers, quietly through the thick water, sober again, and climbed up onto the rocks to sit there as darkness faded, four mermen, happy, deliciously tired, waiting for the sun to come up over the cliffs of The Park and for the old people to appear for their morning swim, and for someone to say, which Pierre did, he said: "Time to sleep," so we swam back to shore, dried ourselves off with our T-shirts, got into Tom's car, and drove home to the flat we shared on Sheinkin Street.

A week after I wrote, Pierre wrote back, an email of three paragraphs of equal size. His message and his tone were angry and unforgiving, there was something mean in his words, as if the fight had never really finished, as if the hurt had not subsided over the years. He didn't mention anything about what had happened between us, didn't respond to my apology. I wondered if, like me, he was still single, if he felt, as I've felt about one or two men in my life, that Turo had been his one chance to be with someone who loved him, and I'd taken that away, destroyed something. Did he want to keep fighting? Was the nasty tone of his message meant as a provocation? But I'll never know, because I did not respond. And that's all there is to say about Pierre.

Time, Place, Body

You'd think you'd remember the first time they inserted a needle into your arm to take blood to see whether you'd live or die. It must have been at a clinic or some laboratory of the Kupat Holim. Blood was taken because blood was where the disease lived and where it began its work. Then you'd wait a week, maybe two, however long it took back then to find out whether you'd be dying a slow undignified death. This was in 1983 or '84, maybe 1985. The news had reached us. A few of us were dying or dead, but the dead were not us. They travelled, had lovers in New York, although I'm not exactly sure what I thought back then. Like now, I fucked around a lot, indulged in the Russian roulette of promiscuity. I think we used condoms, unless we were seeing someone on a regular basis. We classified people by how likely they were to infect us. I say that like it's a fact, but I'm not entirely sure it's true.

Have you been tested, we'd ask in the preamble to

penetration. The overly-cautious didn't kiss or suck, there were those who refused to rim. So they took your blood and sent it to a lab and you waited – a week, two – then you'd go back for the results. The first was negative and even now, thirty-five years later, negative means an escape from death, a wriggling out from the clutches of the disease. I worked at the gay switchboard around that time so you'd think I'd remember the procedure, those years of near-death experiences, all mixed up with the war in Lebanon and the terror of inevitable death that was folded into our days.

Nowadays the test takes minutes. Seconds. They send you a kit and you squeeze blood from the pin prick in your finger made with the tip of the needle included in the box along with various tubes, swabs and long earbuds to extract samples (of what?) from your urethra and rectum. Piss, blood and a bit of pooh sent back in the pre-paid package. I don't remember how we did it in Tel Aviv or where we went to get tested to find out if we were going to live or die?

Yossi died.

Noni died.

We all have ideas about ourselves. I'm not the kind of person who... I'm not the sort of person who... we say this about ourselves and think it's true until it's not. Men whose condoms break always seem to be bragging, oh, my dick's so big. So my condom... a few weeks ago... a few days ago my condom broke. It was a Friday and I was with Federico in the sauna. We kissed and fucked and he kept repeating *hostia*, *hostia*, told me to fuck harder. I can hear his voice now as I write, the pleading, the pleasure, the sound of someone giving themselves completely. His skin, the softness of his arse, the weight of his cock, being inside him was delicious, more delicious than usual, so I checked to see if the condom was intact. We continued to fuck, me banging away with a force that might have been mistaken for anger. At some point I needed to rest and pulled out to discover the condom had ripped and become a latex ring at the base and I'm showing him – *mira, mira* – miming what has happened, saying in my basic Spanish something like *se ha roto*.

This thing that I never thought would happen had happened and I'd been fucking an almost stranger with no protection. He wanted more and we tried but I couldn't. It took me a while... days... maybe a week before I realised it was *my* fault, I'd been the one sitting just before that in the day sauna for too long with the condom tucked against my skin. When Federico had come to me later in the showers and made to hug me, I'd moved away. I didn't want this experience to be the one where I became infected. I didn't want, when I looked back on this moment, to think that this man had been the one to bring the virus into my body.

With other men I have taken the risk. Let's say it's about 2014, before Madrid, I'm in London, many years after leaving Tel Aviv. Kaz and I are still having sex every now and then. Let's say it happened on the night he stayed over, before he went hiking in Sweden, out into the tundra on his own with a backpack, tent and sachets of porridge oats. We'd dated for a while. (Just the tip, we say, and at first it's exhilarating to touch someone's arse with the head of your cock.) We're connected by history, Kaz and I, by Europe, by the shit that's happened in that part of the world – Poland, Russia, Lithuania – places our ancestors lived when they lived on the same continent.

I'm not sure how many times we repeated that sweet and unprotected penetration.

It doesn't happen often, we don't do it often, mainly we do it when we trust, when we feel love for someone, and this unprotected gesture is a declaration of love, as if to say: I would die for you. Maybe I'm being overly-dramatic, maybe not. At the time I felt I wouldn't mind dying with Kaz, he was the kind of person I would die with. Not the day-to-day living, but to die, yes. At that moment of holding him from behind and rubbing myself against his crack and him not saying no and then more than the tip. Maybe it didn't happen on that night, maybe it happened earlier. I know men who have taken the risk and things didn't work out so well for them. F, for example, and P, too. I don't take many risks unless you call having sex with a hundred men a year a risk. We use condoms, except that one time a few weeks ago when the condom broke and I realised we'd been fucking without protection.

How do we begin to imagine our lives without the virus?

There was a time when a positive diagnosis equalled an abrupt ending. There was a time when we lived in anticipation of such an ending, where before you knew it, there it'd be: the announcement of your abrupt exit. But I was expecting so much more, you whimper from your hospital bed, lesions on your face and chest, so gaunt, so thin (all your life you've wanted to be skinny), on your back, no strength to move, barely breathing. That's what we lived in expectation of. Terrified of cuts and wounds, anywhere things could seep in or ooze out, terrified of opening ourselves to rupture.

I was in the army at the time and we were at war. From every side, at any moment, it could come, this abrupt exit. Bam and you're gone. I don't remember precisely but it wasn't so much a question of if but when. The only way for it not to happen would be through trickery, a stunt to outwit death. Today we dodged a bullet. The day after, who knows? Yossi didn't dodge it. Noni didn't. There we were, Noni and I, still soldiers, so it must have been a weekend, Saturday, hitchhiking up from Tel Aviv to the nudist beach, walking from the main road through the fields to the narrow strip of sand and the rocks close to the shore that formed little pools where we paddled. There must have been other men, because I don't think we were ever alone in a room. Or maybe we did have sex alone in a room, maybe we dated, or tried to date, like Yossi and I. It didn't happen often with Yossi, but I remember us in bed, I remember his hands on my back. A couple of years later he got sick, or maybe it was months later, and him and I were sitting on the low wall outside a bar called Works, people staring at him, when he told me about the abrupt ending he was about to experience.

Imagine if that was us, you and I dead in 1990, maybe not together, but dying together, me first, then you. Imagine if those were the scenes of our last days, you at 23, me – 28. So what have you done with your life? School, most years spent in a classroom, then the military. Classroom to platoon, head down to get through it. That's how I got through school, through most of my life. Sex was the only place where not, sex has been my refuge. I love that place. But there we were, you and I. The more I loved you the more I hated myself, or do I mean the more you loved me the more I felt untouchable. Touch me. How else am I supposed to know you love me? You gave yourself completely, your whole body you gave and I'd come inside you, quickly, even though I never came quickly, but you were so beautiful and I was so full of self-doubt and we said things to each other only those who'd die for each other say – I love you, I love you – those words and your beautiful body made me come and you'd get up from bed and I'd listen to you shitting it out. Yossi was dead by then. Noni was dead. We thought we were special. By association, because I had you, I thought I was special. If all I'd had were those first 28 years, the 28th one with you, then what? Now I want 28 more to take me to 84. By the time I get to 84, I want to be able to look back on now. Remember 28 years ago, back in 2019, when you lived in Madrid in that apartment with those big windows overlooking the city with mountains in the distance.

Back then, or maybe a bit later, I read books to prepare myself for the story of my exit. I don't know when we all stopped waiting for our abrupt ending, maybe we never did. In a book I read every year for many years, this guy called Timothy loves a man called Jasper and Jasper is a shit, then he dies and soon Timothy will die. The writer died and I imagine Timothy is a version of him if not entirely him. Recently I re-read the book. I was apprehensive, but needn't have been: everything was still beautiful. The writing, the story, sentence after sublime sentence, it's all still there. *Such Times* is still the book of how I would like to make my exit.

But what of the plague's exit? How do you tell a story that has no end in sight, something not happened but still happening. When will the great painting of the plague be made, the *Guernica* of our plague? What would be in the painting of the state of the world hit by this cluster bomb of a virus? Cadavers, dead babies, burnt houses, Princess Diana, ACT UP, KS lesions, Ronald Reagan. We'd include those close-ups of the virus we saw in *Time* magazine, or was it *National Geographic*, lights shining on dots of yellow and aquamarine. What a spectacular performance, drama as seen only in some deep-sea creatures. Purples, greens, such intricate arrangements, the hands of an artist at work, I mean those things don't come into being on their own. An orgy of worms, a tangle of pipes, and in the background a magenta glow which can only mean blood is flowing all around. Years later, I remember reading, as if in a gossip column, that the beauty of the virus in those photographs was fake, the colours painted in.

I want to say I remember what it was like in those early days of the plague, 1984, '85, this thing in the distance, approaching. I'd just moved to Tel Aviv, still had a year in the army, and the storm in the distance was raging. Foucault had died. Ryan White was being written about. We knew it was a gay disease, that's how it was spoken about and if you were gay, you were on its path of destruction. When I came out to my parents in 1984, I wonder if they thought, as I came out to them, that this son of theirs was a prime target on the warpath of this disease.

My introduction to Tel Aviv was through Noah. He was a medic on our base up in Lebanon. He said I had to meet O. You have to meet him! O. lived in the same small town, and I fell in love the way you do with a first lover, mainly because you've been waiting so long to be in love you'll love anyone, though there was a lot to love about O. He looked good with a cigarette. He played guitar and sang Joan Baez songs, and in his small smokey bedroom we listened to Pat Metheny and Everything But the Girl. He introduced me to his friends in Tel Aviv. One of those friends was Noni and we had sex together, a few of us, and it was great until O. said stop begging everyone to fuck you. It's embarrassing.

I've made my way up to the sauna through Acacias, climbing El Rastro to La Latina, to Callao, and along the edges of Malasaña. Usually I stop for tea before I go in, sometimes at the café with the generous portions of sponge cake, or the Argentinian bakery, but more recently, Rodilla on Calle San Bernardo where there's always a free table to sit at while the tea brews, and I'll eat a brownie, and all the while there's anticipation in my body, the knowledge that soon I'll be amongst naked men, and there'll be only that, bodies and desire, no shame, not for a second, and even if it's dark and the air thick with sweat and smoke, it'll be like being on the beach, running on the sand into the waves, wanting only this body and this body, bodies so close to you (remember how close we were?) and this freedom, complete and open freedom that keeps getting thwarted by a plague that wants to take everything away.

One expects it to come at some point, especially if one keeps fucking around the way I do, randomly and often, with men like this one kneeling before me, opening his mouth to take me in, as if this is his reason for being here and I'm not his first nor his last. Two more men join us, clearly drawn by the kneeling man, as if an eager acolyte bestows on one a special status in this place's hierarchy of worth. One of the men reaches for my nipples while the Swede (we've met before) offers his arse to be fingered.

"I'm on PrEP," he'd said a couple of weeks ago in his accented English.

"What language do you speak?" I asked.

"English," he said.

"Yeah, but what else?"

"Swedish" he said.

"Förlåt," I said, because I'll only do it with a condom.

He smiles at the förlåt but he's not entirely happy. The man expects to get what he wants, flaunting his body there in the dim labyrinth of the sauna, butt exposed, towel in hand over his dick, or not entirely over, because the base of the thick shaft is there for all to see. How nice it would have been to slide into him, to let go. Is that what PrEP does, lets you slide into someone? To be able to put yourself into someone and not worry about the virus – a joy remembered from days gone by – now, *that's* a superpower.

Three men standing and one on his knees on a Saturday afternoon in November. Not a bad thing to be doing almost 40 years – to the day, to the day – since the men at The Everard, at St. Mark's, at the 21st Street Baths, did such things. Four men in this picture of pleasure, two of us already alive back then, back when the plague was born, me and the guy into nipples, but the other two not even born at the birth of the plague, not even conceived in 1985.

Ten minutes in, and there's just about so much cocksucking one can do on one's knees on the cold sticky floor in the semi darkness (*en la oscuridad*) of the sauna on a Saturday afternoon. *Shabbes! Shabbes!* the ancestors chant as they watch the man rise from his knees and walk away without a kiss, without wanting a thank you, a hug, a hug would be nice, or to be told that for those minutes of cocksucking: *dios mío*, ten out of ten, *cariño*!

We did live more innocent lives back then, simpler, our days regimented by chores in the office on the military base, but the evenings were ours, from late afternoon until the next morning we were free to do whatever we wanted. Soldiers got cheap cinema tickets, and if you were in uniform, you got in for free to see concerts at the Mann Auditorium, so we'd turn up in uniform and change into civilian clothes in the bathrooms. Movies, music, and on Friday nights we'd go dancing at Divine on Dizengoff Street. To remember the early years of the plague is to remember all this. 1985, '86, '87.

Noah was there, and I'm not sure who else, but there were probably four or five of us. Someone had a car and we drove the short drive from the club to the beach. I want to say this was before I met C., the English guy L. introduced me to. I think this night I'm thinking about was before then, although there was a night with C. when we walked down to the beach and along the rocks and had sex with the lights of Tel Aviv shining onto us and Lebanon in the distance, further up the coast, where I'd first met Noah – yes, it was his car we were in after dancing all night at Divine.

Where is everyone? Where are they?

If any of us was on the plague's radar, it would have been Noah, the wild one, the romantic, always with young men in love with him, having fun, which seemed to be exactly what the plague didn't want us to be having.

Fun increased your chances of an abrupt ending. It took me another twenty years to really start having fun, to become the sauna whore I am today, but by then – don't jinx it – we'd come up with ways to protect ourselves, to prolong our time. Armed with condoms and luck, I have shielded myself from the plague, kept myself alive.

In this version of the story, nobody dies. There is no plague, no disease. In this version there is no fear. Fear is banished, worry is gone, no plague to plague us. For all our adult lives there is no plague, no fear, no disease.

Ha! says the plague. Watch me shape your love, every touch, kiss, lick. I've shaped it. Whatever you are, I've made you. Try stopping me and I'll find ways in through doors no bigger than pin pricks. I'm the maker of clichés, purveyor of fine hackneyed images, perfecter of the stereotype of the sick homosexual, the dying queer. You think you've got me cornered. I lurk in blood, in cum, in shit. Veil me with medication, silence me with pills, pretend I'm not there, but I wait. Devastation is the least of my plans. Oh, they say, we see an end in sight, we see the weakening. But I'm gaining strength. I see your tricks. I see you. Come, let's swim through this underworld of corpses, surf the tidal wave of loss and fear and memory. I'd name numbers but you wouldn't believe me. Can you believe it! If I told you the story of every body I've wiped from the face of the earth we'd be here till death do us part, even if you were to live forever. Lurking is my superpower, I'd add invisibility, but you see me in every drop of blood, every glimmer of pre-cum, every kiss, cough and *apchee*. Remember how scared you were of a kiss? Any moment with anyone, stranger, lover, arsehole, cock, mouth, finger, nipple, I lurk in unexpected places and then bam! I'm in you. Before you know it we're united and you're proof that good things come to those who wait. I've waited for this, waited a long time to carry myself from this beautiful body into yours. Hello, handsome.

I don't keep up with news of the virus. If you asked me whether people are still getting it back in London, how many cases there are each year, I'd have no idea. I don't really know what PrEP is. Not really. I don't want to know. Knowing opens you up to all sorts of things. Knowing means you might need to know. You'd think someone like me would want to know, but I don't. I don't want that kind of freedom. I don't want drugs to keep me going. Give me the cure or nothing. I carry those years of plague and war with me, the certainty of an abrupt ending. I've lived in a war zone for a long time, stuck in the panic of my 1980s self, shell-shocked. Science has moved on, there have been developments, but have there really, I mean really really, because I'm sure if there had been, someone would have told me.

When I first had sex, protected sex was not on the agenda. I remember shit on my dick. We were on a beach and I washed it off in the sea. This was in 1980 so the Cuban missionary in our small town (what was he doing there?) could have been HIV positive. How I wanted to be seduced. All I wanted in those years, especially then, was to have sex, and if he'd had the virus, I'd have been dead by the summer of 1981, one of the young ones seduced at sixteen, dead by seventeen. Dead without a single taste of good sex, because what are the chances that a boy of sixteen was having good sex with a man who got teenagers to fuck him in the dunes, un-douched, so that when the boy took his dick out it was coated in khaki-brown shit. Or the guy in the jeep, that old Italian guy who asked the seventeen-year-old in his son's high-school class to fuck him.

I left that small town when I went into the army. I was stationed in Lebanon and in the Negev desert, but at some point I managed to get out of that unit and was transferred to a clerical job on a base outside Tel Aviv. I moved to Tel Aviv, which is where I eventually met you in that bar called Works a year or two after Yossi and I had sat on the low wall outside and he'd told me he'd soon be dead.

Later, when you and O. slept together, I left Tel Aviv and moved to London and for those first years in London I was bereft, raging, alone, the way I am some days now in Madrid. It's nice here, despite the interruptions keeping me from writing, cutting short every line as it begins to form, except that's not entirely true. I've written this while being distracted by other things: teaching, drawing, a crazy landlord, lawyers, learning Spanish and Arabic, along with things you do when you're a single person and don't have anyone to – oh, whatever! – I don't want to tell the story of how you and O. had sex. The story of you is tied up with the story of that place, a place that was home, even if it's not where I'm from, and which I'm reminded of here in Madrid in summer, especially when I go to the outdoor pool not far from my apartment, and I lie on the grass in the extreme heat, around me so many beautiful people, talking and laughing the way they do here, loudly. If I had the time I'd tell you in great detail about how much I love those minutes in the locker room, changing into my swimming shorts, then looking for a place to spread my towel on the grass. I'd describe the women who don't cover their breasts, how beautiful and tanned they are, all of them so beautiful, you should come and stay for a few days because I remember how much you loved the heat, how you'd sit in the car with the windows closed in the middle of a Tel Aviv heatwave, in your suit, in that heat that was a nightmare to me, sweating, never able to forget my body, and yet now I'm in my element when it's 40°, lying here on the grass with my body so open, every pore open, and it's like I don't have to wrap up, don't have to put my arms around myself and I can be open, exposed, everybody exposed in the midday sun, every pore calling out for the heat to enter, deep into our blood, our bones, until the heat is so intense and I get up and walk towards the pool, to one of the chrome ladders by the edge, and gradually, carefully step in – watch me slide in – almost naked, into the cool, cool welcoming water.

Madrid, November 2019

A Sea of People

Sometimes when the tide is out you can find men on the shore below Gabriel's Wharf building castles in the sand. M has come down to the river where the breeze cools the air and takes the edge off the heat that has settled over London. One of the sand sculptures is in the shape of a mermaid, the other looks like a sofa and the men recline on it and chat to passersby who stop at the railings and throw coins into a crater as if into a wishing well. Thud. Thanks. Waving. Move on. M gives nothing. He's in awe of anyone with the skill to build couches on the banks of a river in the few hours it takes for the tide to turn and the water to rise again.

Give.

But the thought of throwing, missing, saying the wrong words, being too shrill, being thanked, having to smile... His nails dig into his palms. His lower back is tight. The weight of the world. Sharp and unbending.

Acclimatised now to the grey drizzle of England, this

intense heat is disorienting, three days of it, flinging him back to places he has lived. Deserts. Heat so intense it feels like home, temperature itself is memory. A friend says: Take the day off. A few days. It's not like you're writing anything anyway.

Recently back from a week in Barcelona, M had been caught off guard by the heat in London. After the intensity of Catalonia, he'd expected to return to the unpredictable chill of England. Extreme summer is the exception, a novelty, throwing the city off its course. On the Tube down to the river, Finsbury Park to Green Park, the Jubilee Line to Waterloo, signs advising passengers to carry water, to stay hydrated. People need to be taught how to behave in high temperatures. Twenty years in the city and he's still happiest as a tourist, doing touristy things, meandering, mingling in crowds, walking along the river. Alone, away from his street in North London, his flat, hunched over a desk as if the arc of his body could protect his inner organs, his heart, but this is the posture that brings the pain, a rigid curving of the spine. Here by the river he begins to fuse with the city, it's a kind of disappearance, a participation in the phrase a sea of people.

There are parts of London he associates with sex. For a long time Shoreditch was one of them, there in East London, far from where he is now. A couple of times a month M would go to the bathhouse just off Great Eastern Road, sometimes after teaching a class near Liverpool Street, English to Speakers of Foreign Languages, or after dinner with a friend at Wagamama in Spitalfields Market. In the absence of a man to return to, he'd go to the bathhouse as a way of ending the day in the arms of another. Whenever he is close to a bathhouse, this is always the option. For most people, the option arises in the confines of their home, for M, certain structures around London offer up opportunities for sex: in Vauxhall, Shoreditch, Covent Garden, Oxford Street and here in Waterloo beneath the railway arches, just a short walk from the river.

M called ahead to book a massage with the resident masseur. He will lie on the table, flat on his stomach, arms above his head. The room will vibrate with each train passing overhead, carrying people in and out of London, to Sevenoaks, Gravesend, Folkestone. Lately, when M wants to be touched deeply, the hands he longs for are the masseur's, Piotr, a Russian in London, working quietly or, when he does speak, making inane remarks.

How have you been? M will say.

Shit, Piotr says, warding off questions as if they were lewd advances.

M knows that Piotr, known as Pete, left Moscow in his early 20s, maybe earlier, and moved to – where was it – Chicago? First Chicago, then Spain, no, Ireland. Dublin. The man's English is fluent, though his accent is so thick it's comical: the expectation is a pairing with bad grammar, limited vocabulary, but the Russian masseur makes no mistakes.

While waiting for his massage, M had hooked up with a lean German in the dry sauna, the kind of lean M likes. Even when M himself was young and lean, young and lean had appealed to him, though he'd never have used those words to describe himself. It had taken him years to pluck up the courage to come to a place like this, and still, ten years later, he feels a sense of liberation and triumph, a feeling confined to these rooms, to this space, as if this is where his true self emerges. Mainly he's here for the sex, but today it's the massage. The back pain has persisted since his trip to Barcelona.

"What's your name?" he'd said to the lean German between kisses.

The name is pronounced Mischail. He'd moved to Berlin from Wuppertal, now he's in London for the weekend, spending the night in the sauna – he pronounces the word sour-nah – until a room becomes available in a friend's house in Camden. M tells him that thirty years ago, he'd had a lover who took him to see Pina Bausch in Tel Aviv. The German is surprised to find an enthusiast of modern dance in a place like this. He tells M he loves loves *loves* Pina Bausch, that she was a hero in his town. Him and his best friend used to go and watch her rehearsals in the Wuppertal theatre after school.

"I haven't seen any modern dance for years," M said.

"What did you do in Tel Aviv?"

"Good question," M said.

The memory of that lover is weightless. That's how long it's been. The lover had moved to San Francisco and still lives there with a man he met on a bus in Nicaragua. M went to visit them once and they'd driven up – or was it down? – Highway 1 and stayed overnight in a log cabin on a campsite in the forest. All this floats languidly through M's mind as he enjoys the masseur's touch and thoughts of the German on the ledge beside him.

This is where we are in history, M thinks. Friends are moving back to where they came from, or away: Sicily, Israel, Greece. Europe is reshuffling its people, you go here, you – here, some outwards to the old colonies, Angola, Brazil, the Portuguese are doing it, others from there are arriving in cities like this. Last month there'd been a van driving round London with the sign: *Are you here illegally? Go home or face arrest. Text this number to hand yourself in: key in H and O and M and E.* It shattered the illusion that London belonged to no one, a liminal space where the English didn't matter, language didn't matter. Where else could M go? Home is not an option. Wherever he went he'd be lost all over again.

"Lost?" his friend had asked, "or alone?" The friend

had moved back to Greece after twenty years in London.

"Lost. Alone. Same thing," M had said.

It became clear in Barcelona that getting lost was not his thing, not again, not in a foreign language, a foreign city. He needed London for the safety of its island life, the familiarity of its vocabulary, the melancholy weather that echoed his temperament. The relief of English after years in the desert, like diving into cool water, knowing how to swim. But now, twenty years in and he's restless. Had it really been the language he was longing to return to? He cannot bring himself to use the phrase mother tongue. A couple of days before they'd left Barcelona – M for London, his friend back to Athens – they'd climbed Tibidabo, and as on every trip to every city since leaving home, M had asked himself: Could I live here? Is this where I could escape to? But language imposed exclusion, a feeling of inadequacy. M felt so thwarted he wanted to crawl back to the hotel and ask for things in English, this language that was his, lived in for half a lifetime, conducted love affairs in: room service, please, an extra pillow, a taxi, anything to reduce the delay between wish and fulfilment. The one escape is sex, the realm where the body is vocabulary. Men he meets in places like this, pressing up against each other, almost in slow motion, in synch, the way lovers do after months apart, reacquainting themselves, this person they've loved more than anything. The one true one. Kissing gently, the way he and the German had done, tender, tentative, fingertips on ribs. Our lives filled with the question of desire and its limits: to touch and be touched. By whom and where?

Youth is bold and the German had leaned forward to take M into his mouth, just as other men entered the cabin. Two older men. Why not, men are fucking in public, nakedness on show, a lean chap exposing himself, why shouldn't we join in? One of the older men touched a finger straight to it. The German was not averse to touch – offering himself to M – but the old man neither stroked nor waited for an invitation. Straight to it. Brutal. The German removed the hand, and the old man settled back onto the warm wooden ledge, happy to have touched such firm buttocks, watching as the young man surrendered to M.

Go deeper, he says to the masseur, harder.

The masseur laughs. You need a knife to go deeper.

He, too, M thinks, showing signs of psychopathic rage? London does this to us. On a scale of 1 to 10, how angry are you? Earlier, before the German, also briefly, an Englishman had followed M into a cubicle, pushed him, provoked him to be overpowering. He wanted to be pinned to the wall. But then.

"Not so hard," the guy said.

"That wasn't hard."

"Stop."

"I'll show you hard," M said.

"I'm not into this," the Englishman said.

"Are you not?" M said, thinking the guy was teasing.

The Englishman slapped his face. M slapped back.

"I'm really not," the guy said, grabbing his towel. "So, fuck off."

M stayed in the cubicle, locked the door, lowered himself onto the mattress. One option would be to find the man, tell him to think twice before slapping someone. Be careful who you slap, he'd say. Or he'd smile: That wasn't a good start, was it? Let's try again. But he could tell that an olive branch would not be appreciated.

Fear is the aphrodisiac, the life force, lying under the masseur's touch, letting go into this ultimate state of abandon, thumbs pressing into both sides of his spine, C1, C2. Snap. The room vibrates. A train in or out of Waterloo. When M first started coming here, this room had been a steam room, positioned between the two flights of stairs leading up to the cruising area and private cabins. The room is at the heart of the bathhouse. Both flights of stairs lead to the same place, yet each flight descends into a different part of the sauna. At the foot of one flight is the bar, with its chrome tables and barstools; two overweight men had been drinking tea there, a young man sipping from a bottle of Heineken. Just wait there, the man at reception had said, the masseur will come and get you. At the foot of the other flight is the dry sauna, big enough for two or three people: that's where M had met the German.

In the dream he turns up unannounced at a garden party to surprise an ex-lover. The man is surprised, looks uncomfortable, then disappears into the crowded room, called away by friends. M lands up standing next to a North African guy who's chatting away in Russian, refusing to converse in any other language. M speaks to him in Hebrew, so the guy responds in Dutch and M throws back some Afrikaans, triumphant at being able to understand some of what he's saying, so the guy says something in a language M doesn't recognise. They laugh, enjoying this game, as if they could continue playing forever, ping-ponging snippets of language back and forth. M tells the North African in French that he was born in Israel... no, I mean, I was born in South Africa, then I lived in Israel for *quelques années* before escaping to London. The guy was born in Tunisie, then lived in France, then spent a few months on Kibbutz Tzorah. I grew up just a few minutes from there, M says, even though he didn't. It's a lie, but it's the right thing to say if you want the conversation to continue. Weird that the Tunisian, a Muslim, would stay on a kibbutz, but M doesn't ask. The guy says in English: "While I was there I got like two-hundred tattoos." M can't see any, even though the guy is wearing shorts and a T-shirt, one of those ripped faded Ramones T-shirts that an ex-lover used to wear, a Sicilian who went back to live in Catania.

The inside of his mouth is dry, there's spittle on his lips. M turns his head just a fraction to wipe it off on the tissue paper that covers the hole in the table where his chin is resting, his eyes pressed shut. The touch is firm, the masseur's hands in constant motion along the oiled contours of his body, avoiding nothing, teasing, is he teasing, the way he brushes against M's arse-crack, his balls?

"Remember last time," M says, "what we spoke about?" He hadn't planned on saying this but he says it anyway.

"I think you fell asleep," the Russian says.

"Was I snoring?" M says.

"I thought you'd stopped breathing."

"Maybe I did"

The Russian is massaging his inner thighs, his glutes, working his way across his back towards his head, then he's at the top of the table, his middle level with M's gaze.

"So tell me," the Russian says, "what did we speak about?"

"Sex," M says.

"How much did we say?"

"Fifty."

"Good. Very good."

"And we said you'd be naked," M says.

"No problem," says the Russian, and pulls down his shorts.

M pays others to take care of him, clean his flat, make food, run errands, help with paperwork, do for him what he'd happily share the burden of if he had a lover. There is no lover. Now, on his back, exposed like a piece of meat, no, like a work of art: the table is the canvas and he – layers of impasto. In Barcelona he'd gone to the Antoni Tàpies gallery alone (his friend had gone shopping at El Corte Inglés) and been amused by the exhibition with the desk bolted to the wall, the canvas placed on a straight-backed chair, thought about the difference between the contents of a gallery and the contents of a book. If on a wall is art, then between covers is a book. That which is mounted is art. Put a table on a wall, a box in a frame, hang a sack from the ceiling, turn your painting to the wall, nail planks to a frame. Whatever. It's art. But what to put in the book? The weight of the world.

"That's nice," M says.

The Russian's grip is firm, a fantasy of waking to hands like his pressed into M's flesh. Be in the moment, there's nothing to distract, no one is watching. M is now a man who goes for a massage and gets a happy ending. He is the client. This is what happens, fifty pounds and he's entitled to touch: torso, buttocks, the Russian's tiny balls and soft penis. Unsure how much is included in the fee, yet emboldened by the transaction, M rests his hand on the crack between the masseur's arse-cheeks. Conflicted. Alone. He cannot let go, he won't, M will not give, hold back, keep what he can to himself. This is how he stays whole. To relinquish would be to re-enter the world with nothing. He declines the offer of a hand-job, thanks the masseur, *spasiba*, words gleaned from lovers along the way, like *idi syuda*, *idi domoy*, like *shto ty khochesh*, *kotory chas*. They are the same height, though the Russian is broader, bench-presses heavier weights, wants to be huge, he says, when M pats his chest. Like you, he says to M, joking, putting himself down. He is the kind of handsome that people turn to look at. M cannot imagine him outdoors, though, visiting friends, having dinner. He knows he shares a house with eight men, migrants who come and go. The Russian does not encourage a hug. No, he says, the oil, and opens the door for M so that he can go and fetch the cash from his locker to pay for the groping that went on in that room.

Passing the bar on his way to the showers, M catches the bartender's eye. Isn't he...? He's seen him before, not here, but recently. Somewhere. The bartender looks without hunger, which doesn't mean there isn't any. Good-looking men are cautious in these places. Later he will learn that Esteban has been in the city for six months, got the job because his flatmate is a cleaner here. How much longer he can stick it out in this cave, he doesn't know, not to see sunlight all week, no mobile reception to check comments on the photographs he uploads. Tripod set up near Waterloo Bridge as the sky turns from orange to pink to purple. And then, just as he's leaving, the man with the notebook on the bench, the same guy walking past the bar, the thick chest, the towel across his buttocks, the slow, purposeful gait. I saw you, he'll say to him later.

London has spilt out of its terraced houses, its bedsits, its hotel rooms. Here by the river, crowds do what they've been doing for centuries on balmy nights. The tide has returned, sandcastles have been washed away. The thick air reminds foreigners of home, and for these past few days, and this evening in particular, the damp of the city is forgotten, its grey forgotten, the struggle that is the mainstay of existence – that, too, is forgotten. Surrender to the heat and make this city home. The last London heatwave had been two or three years after M arrived in the city – more than fifteen years ago! – still obsessed with its greenness, such a contrast to the places he'd come from, places with so little of it. Deserts. During that hot summer, he'd made regular visits to the overgrown cemetery on Church Street in Stoke Newington, sat amongst the fern bushes and plane trees, sketched and written, grafted himself onto the city.

The man on the bench next to him reads a book, a man at the railings talks on his phone. A mother and a pram. A woman and a mauve handbag. A jogger in a pale yellow T-shirt. This sea of people. A pigeon on the paving stone. Three pigeons in a row, hello! A kid says: "Let's play so they're not allowed to touch the ground," and they shoo the birds upwards to keep them from landing. A girl in a pink pyjama suit plays with her mother's crutches. And then these two idiots plonk themselves down on the bench beside M – where did the man and his book go? – and now, alone, his defiance is in his grumbling. A solitary man rages: that's his power. The way the English plonk themselves down on benches without a simple may-we, as if the bench were land. Plonk. But the one alone needs to breathe. Such rage, M tells himself, you're only angry because there's no potential for love in this situation. Raging is a toxic form of relating. His friend's voice.

Funny, M thinks, smiles. I should have let the Russian finish me off, should have looked for the German.

"I saw you," Esteban says, there with his camera and tripod.

From behind the bar, now here.

"And I saw *you*," M says.

"Was it good?" Esteban says.

"It was," M says. "And for you?"

"No," Esteban says, then: "Do you like ice cream?"

Pointing to the bus parked on the embankment, a bright pink double-decker converted into a frozen-yoghurt stand, a glorified ice cream van. Young students are handing out pink vouchers to exchange for free samples, pinnacles of frozen yoghurt in shot-size paper cups, an amount easily gulped whole into the mouth.

M and Esteban are, for these moments, tourists in the city, standing at the railings sampling flavours: peanut butter, raspberry, blueberry. They watch the barges, the lights, the clock above the Savoy approaching midnight, the water rising, a seagull on the surface abandoning itself to the river's current. Esteban points his camera at M, tells him to smile. Around them the entire city is awake, intent on participating in this heatwave, or uneased by it, tossing and turning with memories and longing.

M smiles for the camera.

"Careful," Esteban says, pointing to the water that's leaking over the edge of the wall, just a trickle, making a puddle at their feet.

They move away from the railings but the water moves with them, creeping along the embankment. The kids have lost interest in the pigeons and are taking off their shoes to skip in the expanding puddles, half an inch, an inch, like a paddling pool, people laughing, relieved to be cooling their feet, rolling up their trousers as the water rises, lifting their skirts, looking at each other, can anyone explain what's happening? Phones out to take pictures, an event for tweeting and retweeting, every moment a potential once-in-a lifetime. The water flows across the walkway into the skateboarders' pit behind them. The young men move to higher ground, hold onto their boards, jump between concrete bollards as if crossing stepping stones. Everyone's moving to higher ground, the woman with the crutches balances on a bench with her daughter.

"*Vamonos*?" Estaban says.

"Not yet," M says, the water now at their ankles, their shoes in their hands.

It's cold and fresh and it keeps rising.

"I'm going in!" one of the skateboarders says, throws down his board, takes off his shirt, then dives. People laugh and cheer.

The young girl in pink shouts mummy, can I swim, and the mother looks over at M and Esteban and they shrug and smile, what can you do? and the little girl stretches her arms above her, hands clasped together, and launches herself into the cool moving water.

The river covers everything, submerging chairs and café tables outside the National Theatre, people streaming out like balloons being released, like in that YouTube video M had watched where millions of shade balls are released into a reservoir to keep the water from evaporating. We are the shade balls, he thinks, we'll cover the water's surface! Him and Esteban lift with the water as it rises towards the bridge. Boats from the middle of the river steer towards the edges to help those who don't want to swim, hoisting them onto the deck. The bronze lion heads on the opposite bank smile, pigeons hop along the ledge, office workers on a clipper boat for Richmond raise their glasses of white wine. A man in a suit dives in. The serious swimmers take it seriously. At last! A race along the Thames. Race you to Canary Wharf, race you down to Battersea. Buses stop on Blackfriars Bridge and passengers join those standing at the edge looking down, deliberating whether to rescue or join the swimmers. Someone in the water shouts to a couple standing on the ledge: Jump!

And so, roaring with delight, M and Esteban jump.

Everyone is swimming, paddling, floating, from one bank to the other. This is how you cross a river. Even the woman with the crutches is swimming, hallelujah, as if the water is rising to heal the citizens of this broken town. On the rooftops all around, silhouettes of people above Somerset House and St Paul's, the Savoy and the buildings next to it. Everything is reflected in the water, the shapes, the lights, the buildings, bridges became ovals, the Shard – a diamond. We're definitely not drowning, none of us, all of us are being lifted above these streets, moving between structures, peering through windows as we swim past, as if we're flying, all finding a way to stay afloat, holding on, hitching a ride, laughing, egging each other on, you can do it, you can do it, heading for dry land but also avoiding it, letting go into the cool constant pull of the current, all of us here in this city, calling out to each other, waving. All of us. Waving.

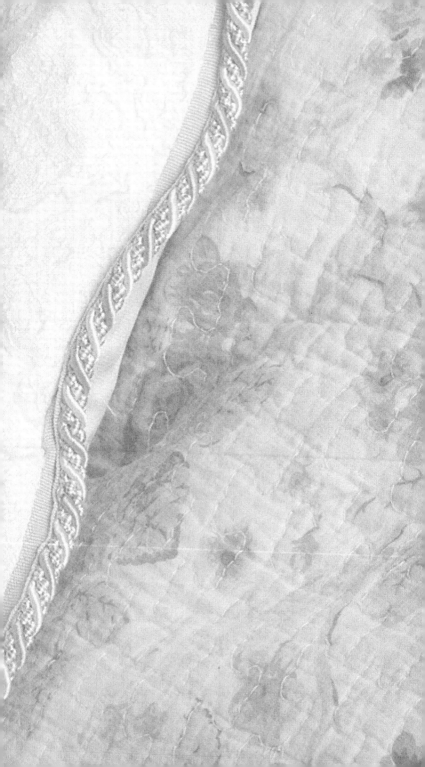

Printed in Great Britain
by Amazon